Perijee & Me

About the author

Ross Montgomery started writing stories as a teenager, when he really should have been doing homework, and continued doing so at university. After graduating, he experimented with working as a pig farmer and a postman before deciding to channel these skills into teaching at a primary school. Author of *Alex, the Dog and the Unopenable Door* and *The Tornado Chasers*, Ross has been shortlisted for the Costa Book Award and nominated for the Branford Boase Award. He is also working on his first picture book, *The Building Boy*, which will be published in 2016. *Perijee & Me* is his third middle-grade novel. He lives in Brixton, London, with his girlfriend, a cat and many, many dead plants.

Also by Ross Montgomery

Alex, the Dog and the Unopenable Door
The Tornado Chasers

Perijee & Me

Ross Montgomery

ff

FABER & FABER

First published in 2016
by Faber & Faber Limited
Bloomsbury House,
74–77 Great Russell Street,
London WC1B 3DA

Typeset by M Rules

Printed by CPI Group (UK) Ltd, Croydon CR0 4YY

The right of Ross Montgomery to be identified as
author of this work has been asserted in accordance with
Section 77 of the Copyright, Designs and Patents Act 1988

A CIP record for this book
is available from the British Library

ISBN 978–0–571–31795–0

FSC
www.fsc.org
MIX
Paper from
responsible sources
FSC® C101712

2 4 6 8 10 9 7 5 3 1

For Rael

My best moment with Perijee happened when we were lying out in the cove. There weren't any clouds that night, not one. If you opened your eyes wide enough you could see all the stars together, looking down on us like a city in the sky. It was just me and Perijee and the waves coming in and nothing else for miles and miles. The sky had never looked so big to me before.

I tried to find one of the stars that Dad had told me about, so I could show it to Perijee. He was still about my size then. This was before he tried to take over the world etc.

'Perijee,' I said, pointing up. 'Look.'

Perijee looked at my finger.

'No,' I said, pointing harder. 'Look *there*. At that star.'

Perijee grew a finger on his hand and tried

to show it to me. I groaned.

'*No*, Perijee.' I pulled his head down to my arm. 'That star, at the end of my finger, is called *Sirius*. It's the closest one to Earth – that's why it's so bright. See?'

Perijee nodded.

'Maybe that's where you came from,' I said.

Perijee glowed, like a candle in a jar. He grew more fingers, tens of them, wrapping round my hands and wriggling.

'Home,' he said.

I smiled. 'That's right, Perijee! *Home!*'

(I felt a bit bad, actually, because right then I realised Sirius was way off in the other direction and I'd been pointing at the wrong star the whole time. It might have even been a plane. I don't think Perijee noticed, so it's no big deal.)

We stayed like that for hours, him with his head on my shoulder and the waves hissing at the stones by our feet and his whole body glowing and fading like a nightlight, while I made up the names of the stars.

'That's the Jam Tart. And that's the Angry Horse. And that's the, er ... Flying Fish.'

Perijee listened until he fell asleep, and when it

was properly late I carried him back across the beach in my arms and laid him in the hut by the jetty and tucked him under the nets.

It was my most special moment out of all the times we spent together, easy. Because as I stood there in the middle of the cold, dark hut and watched him sleep, I realised for the first time how *small* he was. Even though he was my size.

He didn't look like an alien at all. He looked like a baby.

And right then I knew that no matter what happened to Perijee and me, no matter how much we changed, it was my job to make sure that he was always safe and always loved and always happy.

Otherwise, what's the point of being a sister?

It all started just like any other morning, except I was holding a pineapple and the cove was covered in ten thousand dead jellyfish.

The cove wasn't normally covered in dead jellyfish. Normally it was covered in shingle, which is like rubbish painful sand. It was pretty much the only thing there was on Middle Island – that's why no one else lived there, apart from me and Mum and Dad.

By the end of that day, lots of other things would be different – in fact, everything would be. But I didn't know that then. All I knew was that I had a pineapple.

Frank's boat finally appeared, creaking through the cove in a cloud of smoke.

'You're late!' I shouted.

Frank was always late. He made me miss the

school register so often the others in class had started calling me 'Late-lin' instead of Caitlin, which is my name. When I asked if they could call me something else, they changed it to 'the weirdo who just moved here and who can't read or write properly', which is what they stuck with for the rest of the year.

Frank used to be a local fisherman, but he wasn't very good at it so Mum and Dad hired him to drive me to school every day instead. He has long hair like a lady and a big bushy beard, and doesn't do any normal grown-up things like own a car or wear shoes.

He stopped the boat beside the jetty and stared out.

'Jesus,' he said.

'It's a pineapple,' I explained. 'We all have to bring in food.'

Frank pointed behind me.

'I was talking about the jellyfish, Caitlin.'

'Oh yeah,' I said. 'Them.'

I climbed into the boat while Frank shook his head some more.

'Never seen anything like it ... Dead fish everywhere, boats wrecked, flooding all over the mainland ...' He turned to me with a grin. 'Some storm, eh?'

'What storm?' I said.

Frank was surprised. 'The one last night, sprat. With all the thunder and lightning.'

I shook my head. Frank frowned.

'. . . And the gale-force winds? The twenty-foot waves? The massive meteor shower that people saw all over the world?'

'That sounds exciting,' I said.

Frank glared at me. 'Yes, Caitlin! It was the biggest storm in years! People thought it was the end of the world! How did you miss it?' He pointed across the cove. 'Look – on the other side of the island there are prawns washed up on the beach that are bigger than . . .'

'Wow!' I gasped. 'You can see *that* far away, even with your . . .'

I suddenly realised what I was saying and stopped. The other thing I should mention about Frank is that he has a glass eye. Sometimes I really want to ask him about it – like if his old one's in someone else's head, so he can swivel it round and look at their brains – but that would be impolite so I never mention it.

'You'd better not be going on about my bloody eye again,' Frank muttered.

The engine belched and we set off for the mainland.

'So,' said Frank after a while. 'Nice pineapple.'

'Thanks!' I said. 'I thought I'd bring in an exciting fruit, seeing as it's the last day of term.'

Frank whistled. 'Summer holidays! Ooh, you jammy git. I'd love six weeks off work.'

'You don't have a job,' I pointed out.

Frank scowled at me. 'What about you? Anything exciting planned for your time off?'

Of course I had. I'd been planning it for *weeks*.

'I'm going to have a party on the island!' I said. 'I'm inviting the whole class today!'

Frank looked amazed. 'Wow! Your parents don't mind having that many people over?'

'I'm sure they won't,' I said.

Frank's smile disappeared.

'. . . You have asked them, haven't you?'

'Of course!' I said. 'I mean, *I will*, eventually. But let's face it – they'll both be too busy to care what I do over the holidays anyway. Dad's not back from his book tour for months, and Mum's got a big deadline so she'll be on the computer every day. Even more than usual.'

Frank shifted nervously beside me.

7

'Look, sprat – I'm not sure having a party is such a good idea. Why not just invite a couple of mates over?'

I groaned. 'I've *tried* that! I invite people from my class all the time, but they're always busy – every single weekend! I mean, how am I supposed to make any friends up here if no one ever comes over?' I laughed. 'It's almost like they're making up excuses not to come, because they think I'm a complete dork. Or something.'

We made a big turn in the water and the mainland appeared up ahead. You could already make out the school – it was the biggest building for miles. It had taken a real battering in the storm. There was a dead octopus hanging from the flagpole, and a whale was stuck on the street and blocking traffic.

'But if I invite the whole class at the same time,' I said, 'then someone's *bound* to be free, right? For one day in six whole weeks?' I sighed. 'I mean, if they're not ... I'll be on my own all summer. And that would be *awful*.'

Frank said nothing. We pulled into the harbour and I leapt out.

'Well, see you at hometime!' I said. 'I might be a bit later than normal, because I'll be taking suggestions for cake flavours and ...'

'Caitlin.'

I turned round. 'Yes, Frank?'

Frank thought about saying something, then changed his mind. He smiled instead.

'Nothing,' he said. 'I hope your plan works out. Good luck, sprat.'

I gave him a big grin and ran to school, clutching the pineapple to my chest. I was so excited – I was finally going to make some friends, for the first time ever! It was nice for Frank to say it, but I didn't need any *luck*.

Why would anyone say no to a party?

I left before everyone else when the bell rang for the end of the day and walked quickly down to the harbour. I only stopped to throw my pineapple at a wall and stamp it into chunks.

I was much faster than normal, so Frank was still smoking by the time I got to the boat. He started coughing when he saw me and threw his cigarette into the water.

'Christ!' he said. 'You're in a hurry!'

I got straight in.

'Er . . . everything all right?' said Frank.

I sat and waited. Frank bit his lip, then quickly turned on the engine. We drove off in silence. The waves smacked against the front of the boat and the mainland slipped out of sight behind us. Frank glanced over at me.

'So . . . went well, did it?'

My lip started trembling.

'Oh no,' said Frank. 'Please don't start crying.'

I did. I sprayed tears all over the place. Tears and worse. Frank looked like he was trying to sail through a hurricane.

'Argh ... oh god ... there's bound to be some tissues somewhere ... take the wheel, will you?'

I steered and sobbed while Frank looked for tissues. Eventually he came back with an old tea towel he found under a gutbox.

'Want to talk about it?' he said gently.

I shook my head. 'You wouldn't understand. Schools were completely different when you were my age. They hadn't even discovered electricity.'

Frank frowned. 'I'm forty-two, Caitlin.'

'You'd have had candles instead of computers, and horses instead of ...'

'Just tell me what happened.'

My eyes filled up again.

'They all laughed at me,' I said quietly. 'The whole class. No one wants to come over.' My voice started trembling. 'I've got to spend the whole summer ... *by myself!*'

Right on cue Middle Island appeared up ahead, gloomy and grey with clouds. It looked even more empty than usual. I burst into tears, again. Frank pulled up by the jetty and turned the engine off. We sat and floated in silence, clouds of jellyfish lapping against the sides like bubblebath.

'I'm sorry they laughed at you, sprat,' he said. 'They shouldn't have done that. I know what it's like to be lonely around here. Some days you're the only person I talk to, apart from the fish.'

I looked at him suspiciously. '. . . You talk to the fish?'

'That's not what I meant,' Frank muttered. 'I mean that I never married or had kids. It's a tough life, being a bachelor at my age.'

I wiped my eyes. 'But you've got friends – you talk about those guys down the pub all the time! And there's *loads* of people where you live on the mainland! On Middle Island it's just me and Mum – and Dad, when he's back from tour . . .'

'Doesn't mean you can't get lonely,' said Frank. He patted me on the back. 'It's going to be tough for me these next six weeks, not seeing your face every morning. I'll miss you.'

I glanced up. '. . . You will?'

'Course I will!' said Frank. 'You're my friend, aren't you?'

I felt like I was glowing.

'. . . We're friends?'

'You bet,' said Frank. 'And I'll be counting down the days until I can see you again.' He stretched out across the bench. 'I'll have to find some other ways to pass all my free time. A few long lie-ins, maybe . . . a little fishing . . . a lazy stroll to the pub around lunchtime . . .'

I leapt onto the bench.

'Then that settles it!' I cried. 'We'll start Monday morning!'

Frank looked blank. 'Start what?'

'Spending the summer together!'

Frank sat up.

'You what?'

'It's the perfect solution,' I explained. 'You're lonely, I'm lonely . . . We can hang out together instead! Every single day! That's what friends do, right?'

Frank was so delighted he'd gone pale. 'But – but—'

'At least that way I won't be so crushingly sad and lonely,' I added.

Frank didn't speak for a long time. When he did, he was gritting his teeth.

'Fine,' he said. 'I'll come over. For one day a week – all right?'

I gasped. 'Really?'

'Yes! Really!' Frank snapped. 'But the *second* you start going on about me taking out my eye . . .'

I didn't even let him finish. I gave him the biggest hug you've ever seen.

'Frank,' I said. 'I don't care what everyone else says about you – I think you're the absolute best.'

Frank smiled. I couldn't see it, but I could feel it.

I told Frank to come on Monday at dawn. He wasn't too happy about it, but I insisted we start early so he could make me breakfast. I ran all the way home and charged straight into Mum's study.

'Mum!' I said. 'Guess what! I . . .'

She was still in her pyjamas. She didn't even move when I came in – just kept staring at the screen, typing. The cup of tea I'd made her that morning was still there, untouched.

'Mum,' I said again.

She turned round like I'd just spoken. She looked tired, as usual.

'Oh,' she said. 'Sorry, pickle. I was miles away.'

Mum is a *marine biologist*. That's someone who knows everything there is to know about life in the sea. She used to work on a boat in the middle of the ocean, right above the Mariana Trench – the really deep bit, where they find fish with lightbulbs on their heads.

But when we moved to Middle Island, Dad made her give up her job. He's an *astrobiologist* – someone who knows everything there is to know about life in space. He's written books about it, big thick ones with his name and face on the front. He started doing book tours that went on for months, so Mum had to stay at home to do his paperwork for him.

'How was your last day at school?' she said, rubbing her eyes. 'Did your friends like the pineapple?'

I hadn't got around to telling Mum the truth yet – that I didn't actually *have* any friends. But I couldn't tell her now. When Mum's busy, she gets upset at the slightest thing. The problem is, she's always busy.

I gave her my biggest, widest smile. 'They loved it!'

Mum sighed. 'Oh good. You should invite them all over one day in the holidays.'

I smiled even wider.

'Good idea! Funnily enough, I was just talking to Frank about that, and he said . . .'

'Did you get your report?'

My smile fell like a cheap shelf.

'R . . . report?'

Mum turned her chair round to face me.

'Your *end of term* report, Caitlin,' she said. 'The one that says how well you've been doing at school.'

My mouth went dry. I wasn't doing well at school – at all. In fact, I was the worst in class by miles and miles.

I hadn't got around to telling Mum *that* yet, either.

'I still can't believe it, darling.' She smiled proudly. 'My little Caitlin, *top of the class!*'

I gulped. 'Er ... yeah.'

'You must have worked so hard!'

I had. It's not easy, lying that much.

I've had the same problem ever since I was little. Whenever I look at a book the letters flash and change in front of me like traffic lights. The moment I think I've got a word pinned down, it slips away from me again. It's like trying to learn an alien language – one that everyone understands except me.

'I mean, it makes *such* a difference from your last school,' Mum continued. 'All those meetings about your reading and writing problems, and your father having to argue with your teachers about your test results, and those extra sessions he paid for so you didn't repeat the year ...'

My face burned. I didn't need any reminding about *that*.

Mum and Dad just don't get it. They're both so smart, they think it's *normal* to be like that. Every room in the house is filled with essays and framed certificates and big, heavy science books that I can't even lift – let alone *read*.

'So where's the report?' said Mum excitedly. 'Can I see it?'

I thought lying would make my life easier – but I was wrong. At first it was just a little fib here and there, to stop Mum from worrying about me. But then one lie had led to another, and they'd grown and grown, until soon I was telling lies so big I had no idea how to stop them. Now I was dropping letters from school over the side of the boat every day, and burying all my homework in the back garden so Mum couldn't see my bad marks ...

But my report was different.

'It's being posted,' I said emptily.

Mum sighed. 'Oh, I can't *wait*! We should send your father a copy when it arrives, too.'

I felt the ground cave in under me.

'You know how much he cares about your schoolwork,' Mum added.

I swallowed. 'Yeah. Great idea.'

I must have looked as miserable as I felt, because suddenly Mum stopped smiling. She squeezed my shoulder.

'I know he's tough on you,' she said. 'Your father isn't the easiest person to live with. But he just wants you to do well. And now you're finally getting good marks ... well, it makes moving up here and giving up my job worth it. I'm so proud of you, Caitlin.'

My heart sank. I couldn't stand lying to Mum. Right then, I would have given *anything* for a distraction.

The phone rang.

'Going out!' I screamed. 'Love you!'

I was out the house and across the fields before Mum could say another word. I breathed a sigh of relief – I'd done it again. I'd bought some time before she and Dad found out the truth. But not much. The report was coming and there was no way I could stop it.

I shook my head – it didn't matter. I'd think of some way to hide it when it arrived. I'd say it got lost. Or maybe I could even forge a copy with good marks written on it ... but of *course* I couldn't do that. My writing was almost as bad as my reading!

I groaned. How was I going to look Mum and Dad

in the eye and tell them that I was the worst in the year at *science* . . . ?

Squelch.

I was standing knee-deep in thick black mud.

'Ugh!'

Middle Island isn't all shingle beaches and no houses. Oh no. I forgot to mention the disgusting, smelly bogs that cover the rest of it. You can usually walk over them if you're careful, but all the rain from the storm had made them like walking on jam. Only not delicious.

I heaved myself out the mud. The whole island ahead was waterlogged. But I couldn't go back home now – not when Mum wanted to talk about my report. I had to stay out until she was busy again. And the only other place I could get to from here was . . . Stinky Bay.

'UGH!' I groaned.

I call it Stinky Bay because it stinks. I named everything on the island when we first moved here. There's also Boring Field, Lonesome Hill, Friendless Cliff, Miserable Pond and The Soli-Tree. I'd tell you the others – but I can't, because that is literally all there is on Middle Island.

Stinky Bay smelled even worse than usual,

because of all the dead prawns heaped along the shore and buzzing with flies. I slumped down on the shingle and threw stones at them.

'Stupid island,' I said.

I remember when we used to live in the city. Our flat was at the top of a massive old building. The woman next door had seven dogs and the couple below us had triplets that screamed all night. It was noisy, but it was nice. I was happy.

Then Dad came home and said that he'd bought a big house on the other side of the country and we were all moving there. I was so excited – my very own island! But Mum wasn't happy at all. Why hadn't Dad checked with her first? What was she going to do about her job?

Dad shook his head – we had no choice. Now he was famous, he needed somewhere quiet to relax after his tours. And besides, he said, we had to get Caitlin into a decent school – one that could sort out her 'academic issues'.

'Stupid academic issues,' I said, throwing stones.

Dad wasn't always like that. When I was younger, me and him used to do stuff together. Go to museums, or the aquarium – but I hardly ever saw him now. Whenever we spoke on the phone, he was always too busy to talk for more than a few minutes. And then when he did come home, all he and Mum did was argue. She'd go up to bed on her own, and he'd sit me down and ask me questions about school, and why I was still doing badly in science, and why was I so lazy, and didn't I want to be a famous scientist like him when I grew up?

That's the problem with you, Caitlin. You don't *understand*. You need good marks to be a scientist. You can't mix up your letters and flip your numbers. You can't be . . .

'Stupid,' I whispered.

I looked up. Night had fallen already. It gets dark here so quickly – you turn around one moment and the sun's gone. I threw a stone into the sea and it disappeared without a trace.

I groaned. This was hopeless. I couldn't spend the next six weeks stuck here by myself, counting down the days until Mum and Dad finally found out the truth. There had to be *something* around here that could fix it, *something* that could help me, *anything* . . .

. . . And just like that, there was Perijee.

He was lying on the stones right in front of me.

He wasn't Perijee yet. Not properly, anyway. This was before he grew up and took over the world. Back then, he was just a prawn.

He wasn't even a proper prawn. He had a shell and two long feelers and he was the same size as a prawn – but he was completely white.

And still, too. *Dead* still.

I crept over to him, a carpet of shingle crunching under my feet.

'Oh wow,' I said.

His shell wasn't like a normal shell at all. It was soft and warm, like candlewax. And there were these *things* all over him, like . . .

'Oh *wow*.'

He was covered from head to tail in letters. Letters I'd never seen before – symbols.

They were carved into him.

He wriggled. I fell over with a scream.

'You're alive!'

He was – barely. He must have been out the water for hours. I quickly wrenched a welly off my foot and dipped it in the sea, then dropped him inside. He lay still in the water for a second – then his feelers twitched.

'Phew!' I said. 'You're OK.'

I looked at him in amazement. I couldn't believe it – I had a pet! My very own prawn! And a special one, too. His shell was white as paper. It might have been the moonlight, but for a second I could have sworn he was glowing.

I ran all the way home in my socks, clutching the welly to my chest. By the time I reached the front door most of the water had slopped out and the prawn was kicking feebly at the bottom. I needed somewhere else to put him, quick.

'The woodshed!'

No one used the woodshed – it was almost falling down. But there was an old metal bucket at the back, full of rainwater and frogspawn. There were already a dozen frogs bobbing around the bottom.

I emptied the welly into the murky water and peered inside. The prawn shone like a star at nighttime.

'Wait here!' I said. 'I'll get you some food!'

I charged into the kitchen and climbed up onto the counters, rummaging through the cupboards. I had no idea what to feed a prawn. Did you have to buy them special food? Or could I just dump a Pot Noodle in the bucket and wait for the water to . . .

'*Caitlin!*'

I swung round. Mum was standing in the doorway, mouth open. She pointed at the floor.

'Where have you *been*?'

I looked down. I forgot my feet were covered in mud. So was the kitchen floor. And the counter. And the breadbin. And the bread.

'Oops,' I said.

Mum put her head in her hands.

'Caitlin,' she groaned, '*tell me* you haven't brought another animal home.'

I tried to look like I didn't know what she was talking about.

'I don't know what you're talking about,' I said.

Mum folded her arms.

'The otter, Caitlin. The one with rabies.'

I blushed. 'Er . . . I don't recall . . .'

'It was last week,' said Mum. 'Like the seagulls.

And the lobster. And the jar of wasps you left floating in the bath.'

I groaned. 'For the last time, they were BEES! Mum, this is completely different, it's . . .'

'I don't care if it's the missing link,' said Mum. 'You can't bring back everything you find on this island.' She pointed to the door. 'Take it back now.'

'But . . .'

'TAKE – IT – BACK.'

She was doing Mum-face. There's no getting past Mum-face. I thought about a million different things I could say to try and convince her, but I knew it was no good. I stormed out the house and slammed the door behind me.

It was so unfair! Mum and Dad wanted me to be good at science, but they never let me do the fun stuff like collecting rat skeletons or building a flamethrower. It was all books, books, books. And anyway – what did Mum care what I did with my free time? It wasn't like I'd be spending any of it with *her* while she sat on the computer all day! I mean for god's sake, I could look after a flipping *prawn* . . .

The woodshed floor was covered in water. The bucket had fallen over.

'Oops,' I said.

The frogs were in a pile in the middle of the shed, scrambling over each other. They were trying to get away from the bucket as fast as they could. Away from ...

Away from the thing crawling out from inside it.

It was the prawn. Sort of. He was still white and covered in symbols.

But he had frog legs.

My mouth hit the floor. 'How did ... how did you ...'

He hopped over to one of the frogs and looked it up and down. Like he was *studying* it.

Then his stomach swelled out, and his eyes bulged, and his feelers disappeared. Soon he was exactly the same as the frog in front of him. Still bright white, still covered in carvings ... but that was it. In every other way, he was a perfect copy.

Then he ate it in one gulp.

I had to steady myself on the door. This was more than a pet. This was the greatest pet in the history of the world. This was a *miracle*.

But whatever he was, he wasn't going to last five minutes in the woodshed. The second Mum found him, he'd get thrown away faster than my Bee Maracas. I needed somewhere to hide him – somewhere safe.

Somewhere no one would look in a million years.

'Caitlin?'

'Yes?'

'What did you do to the guest room?'

I sat bolt upright. Mum was standing at my bedroom door with a face like thunder.

'It looks like you ran a sodding car through it,' she said.

I panicked. I'd shut the frog in the guest room the night before. I figured he was safe in there – I mean, we never had any guests.

'Did you see anything . . . *unusual* when you went in?' I asked.

'I saw the hole you left in the door,' said Mum.

I gawped.

'A *hole?!*'

'A hole.'

I thought about it.

'... How big is the hole?'

'Big enough,' said Mum.

I leapt out of bed and charged past her. She spun round in surprise.

'*Hey ... !*'

I skidded to a stop at the guest room. There was a hole in the middle of the door as big as a football. The frog was gone.

'*Get back here, young lady!*'

I was in trouble – big trouble. But this was too important. With every second, the frog was getting further away. I had to think, fast. I shoved on my woolly bobble hat and yellow wellies, and flew outside just as Mum appeared at the bottom of the stairs.

'*Caitlin!*'

I slammed the door shut behind me. No going back now. There was a path trampled through the fields ahead – it *had* to be him. I ran along it as fast as I could, praying that I wasn't too late, praying that he hadn't managed to get back to the sea already ...

I stopped just before I fell headfirst into the bogs.

There he was, right in front of me. He was stuck in the mud, trying to wrench himself out. He'd grown even bigger overnight – he still *looked* like a frog, but now he was the size of a fat dog. He was absolutely terrified.

'Hey!' I shouted.

He swung round, his eyes wide and scared. I waded into the mud after him.

'Stay there!' I said. 'I'm coming to get you!'

The second I did, he panicked. He started squealing and thrashing his arms around. It looked like he was getting *bigger* too, right in front of me. I waved my hands.

'No!' I said. 'Stay still! If you keep moving you'll sink!'

But he didn't stop. He thrashed and thrashed – and that wasn't all he was doing. His whole body was changing colour, from bright white to purple. He was growing new arms too, springing them out his head and flailing them around while he sank deeper and deeper into the mud ...

I grabbed an arm and pulled him as hard as I could. His head popped out again, spitting and spluttering. But the rest of him stayed stuck in place. It was amazing. I pulled and pulled, and his whole body just stretched out like a bit of gum.

'Wow!' I gasped. 'What are you *made* of?'

He finally came unstuck with a great *shlump*

and we both sprawled back onto the grass. I sat up, panting for breath. He lay on the ground in front of me, plastered with mud, his arms all stretched out and floppy like a big deflated octopus.

'Are you OK?' I said.

He didn't say anything, obviously. He just stared at me with those tiny black eyes – like two full stops on a blank page.

'Look,' I said. 'I'm sorry I shut you in the guest room. I was just trying to keep you safe. I didn't mean to scare you.'

He lay there, his chest sinking like a balloon until he was his old size again. He started slowly turning back to white. I gulped.

'How ... how can you change colour like that?' I murmured.

He said nothing. He looked so helpless.

'Here,' I said. 'Let me clean you up.'

He let me wipe the mud off him. This time he didn't scream or try to run away.

'See?' I said gently. 'I'm not going to hurt you. Just one more bit here and I'm done ...'

I wiped the mud off his chin, and as I did something appeared – like I'd drawn it on with my thumb. A thin black line.

A *mouth*.

'Hey!' I cried. 'How did you ...'

Suddenly he was opening and closing it right in front of me. Then he was on his feet, sucking his extra arms and legs back inside him like spaghetti and stumbling towards me. I fell back, terrified.

'No!' I screamed. 'Don't eat me!'

His tiny dot eyes flickered across my face. A pair of ears popped out either side of his head. Then his skull started stretching up, warping and squidging into a point. A little ball popped out the end.

A *bobble*.

I grabbed my hat in disbelief.

'... Are you *copying* me?!'

He didn't stop. His feet swelled into the shape of wellies. He held up his flippers and started growing fingers on them – two on one, and four on the other. He looked up at me, confused.

'T-ten,' I said quietly, holding up my hands.

He copied slowly, finger by finger, looking up each time to check. Then when he was done he stood in front of me. He was like a tiny, bright white mini-Caitlin.

I was gobsmacked. This wasn't a prawn, or a frog. This was ... something else.

'The meteor shower,' I whispered. 'That was you, wasn't it?'

The alien didn't say anything.

'Er ... OK then,' I said. 'Welcome to Earth, I guess. I'm Caitlin.'

I stuck out my hand for him to shake. He looked at it for a bit. Then he reached out and held it, like I was his mum.

'No,' I said. 'Not like *that*. Like this.'

I tried shaking it, but he didn't get it. He just held on really tight and wouldn't let go. It was quite cute, to be honest. With his drawn-on smile and his hat and his wellies, he really did look like a little person.

Or a brother.

I stopped shaking.

My very own baby brother.

And suddenly, my summer holidays didn't look so boring any more.

I found an old bathtub in a field and covered it with a picnic blanket.

'There!' I told him. 'One comfy, alien-sized bed. You can sleep outside now, seeing as the storm used up all the rain. Now, make sure you don't go anywhere near the house – Mum'll flip if she sees you. She doesn't understand pets. What about food – are you hungry?'

He was. He ate everything I could find – and I mean *everything*. He ate the bark off the trees. He hoovered up the dead jellyfish off the beach like gumdrops. Stones, mud, clothes . . . whatever it was, he swallowed it down and cried for more. I had to stay up all night, sneaking food out the kitchen and carrying it to the bathtub to keep him happy.

I was emptying all the cereal into a pillowcase the next morning when Mum walked in.

'It's not what it looks like,' I said.

'I'm sure it isn't,' said Mum.

I stood frozen to the kitchen counter, waiting for the moment she'd start screaming at me. I hadn't even seen her since running out the day before. She walked over to the oven and hit it with a poker until it worked – everything in the house is broken.

'Caitlin?' she said.

My heart pounded. '... Yes, Mum?'

'Are you happy here?'

It wasn't what I'd expected her to say at all.

'What makes you think I'm not happy?' I said.

'Well, you smashed up the guest room yesterday,' she said. 'And now you're filling a pillowcase with cereal.'

I tried to think of a good reason to be doing either of those things. I gave up.

'I've found an alien on the beach,' I said. 'He was a prawn and then a frog, but now he's a person and he eats everything so I have to get him food.'

Mum thought about it.

'Is this alien the reason there's a whole turkey missing from the freezer?'

'Yes.'

'And was this alien the one who took my best

clothes out the wardrobe last week and put them on the scarecrow?'

I was about to say no, but then I figured I was in enough trouble anyway, so . . .

'Yeah, that was him,' I said. 'He also deleted a load of files off your computer by accident and he's really sorry about it.'

Mum sighed. 'Right. An alien. Thought so.'

She gave me a quick kiss on the forehead and began to walk out. I watched in amazement.

'Wait – that's it?' I said. 'You're not angry with me?'

'Probably,' said Mum. 'We'll talk about it when your father gets back. Just put the pillowcase in the wash when you're done, please.'

And with that, she was gone. I breathed a sigh of relief. I'd told her the truth and she didn't even care! Having a busy mum was actually great sometimes.

I ran to the other side of the island and banged on the bathtub.

'Hey! Alien! Wake up! I got you some more food!' I threw off the blanket. 'You'd better eat this slower than you ate that turkey though, or . . .'

The bathtub was empty.

'Alien?'

There was a sudden *SQUAWK* behind me. I swung round. A flock of seagulls was scattering in the distance. I could just make out a flurry of blood and feathers on the ground below.

'Not again!' I moaned.

By the time I got there, he'd already eaten eight of them. I counted the beaks.

'Stop that!' I cried, slapping a wing out his mouth. 'I told you – no killing things! It's wrong!' I held up the pillowcase. 'Look, I already found some more food . . .'

He launched on the pillowcase mouth first, swallowing it in three big bites like a giant plum. I was amazed. He'd already grown another inch overnight. His bobble came up to my chest now.

'You need to slow down,' I said. 'You understand that, right? *Slow down?*'

The alien looked at me. His smile was in the middle of his forehead.

'Your mouth goes down there,' I said, pointing.

He moved it. I sighed.

'Look – I don't know what I'm doing, OK? I've never had a brother or sister before, let alone an alien. Dad would know how to look after you, but he's not back for *months*.'

'Dad,' said the alien.

'Exactly!' I said. 'He's spent his whole life talking about aliens and whether or not they exist. He'd know *exactly* what to do with you, but . . .'

I stopped. I spun round.

'Did you just talk to me?!'

The alien looked at me, blank. I grabbed him by the shoulders.

'Do it again!' I said.

The alien shuffled his feet.

'D-dad,' he said.

His voice was strange and quiet and croaky, like a bird. But it was a word. I laughed out loud.

'I don't believe it!' I said. 'You talk! What else can you say?'

The alien thought about it.

'Dad?' he said.

I shrugged. 'Well, we can work on that. I can teach you some more words, and then . . .'

I trailed off.

'Oh flip,' I said. *'That's it!'*

I shook the alien in excitement, my eyes shining.

'I'll teach you how to talk!' I said. 'By the time Dad gets back at the end of summer, you'll be able to tell him everything about yourself – where you come from, what type of alien you are … Dad'll be so happy, he won't *care* about my stupid report!'

I turned round to Middle Island. Maybe it was the summer sunshine, or maybe it was the fact that I'd been awake for about twenty-four hours, but it had never looked more beautiful.

'So,' I said. 'Where shall we start?'

'This is a book,' I said.

The alien tried to eat it.

'No!' I said, pulling it out his mouth. 'Books aren't for eating. Especially not this one – Dad wrote it.' I wiped off the spit. 'See? That's him on the front. He writes loads of books, all by himself. He doesn't even use spellcheck.'

I opened it up and looked inside. The words were really small and hard to read. The letters danced and flashed around the page. My head hurt just looking at them.

'These are words,' I said. 'Everything I've said today is words, but these are written-down words.' I pointed to a few different ones. 'That one is ... *D-AR* ... Dark! And that's *M-OOOO* ... Moon! See?'

The alien pointed to a word.

'That's – hang on.' I squinted and jammed my

head right up to the page, sounding out the letters one by one. *'PE . . . RRRRRRRR . . . IIIIIG . . . Oh! That's "perigee".'*

'Peri-jee?' said the alien.

'You won't see that much,' I explained. 'It's when the moon is really close to the Earth. That's why it sometimes looks bigger than normal. And Dad says when it happens, everything on Earth weighs a little bit less, too! Because of gravity, whatever that is. Isn't that cool?' I smiled. 'He knows loads of things like that. He's really clever.'

'Perijee,' the alien murmured, reaching out and stroking a photograph of the moon.

'That's not *actually* the moon,' I said. 'That's just a picture. You'll see the real one tonight.'

The alien bounced up and down with excitement.

'Perijee perijee perijee!' he squeaked.

I smiled. It was nice to see him so happy.

'You like that word, don't you?' I said. 'Maybe that can be your name. It's not a normal name, but then you're not really normal. In fact – I don't even know if you're a boy or a girl. Which one are you?'

'Perijee,' said the alien.

'Yeah, that's just what a boy would say,' I sighed. 'Tough luck. Well, nice to meet you anyway, Perijee.'

We shook.

'Well remembered!' I said. 'Now – what shall we learn next?'

I laid the rocks in a line.

'Three rocks,' I said. 'One, two, three.'

I picked up a rock.

'This is *one*. But if I add this rock –' I picked up the next one, '– it makes *two*. Then if you add this rock, it's *three*. See?'

Perijee picked up the third rock.

'One two three,' he said.

'No,' I said. 'That's one. Remember? *One*.' I gave him two rocks. 'Now – how many?'

Perijee looked confused. 'One?'

'No,' I said. '*That's* one. One and one are *two*. Got it?'

The alien blinked.

'food,' he said.

'No,' I said firmly. 'You just ate that wasps' nest. On this planet we only eat three times a day, and sometimes extra if it's your birthday or no one's looking. Now—' I put the rocks back on the floor. 'How many?'

Perijee looked at the rocks.

'*One two three*?' he said.

'Good!' I hid one behind my back. 'And if I take away this rock – how many are left?'

Perijee thought about it.

'*One two three*,' he said.

'No!' I groaned. 'It's two! Two!'

'*One two three*,' said Perijee, and ate the rocks.

'There!'

I finished carving the word into the ground.

'That's your name. See?'

I pointed to it with the stick. I had written:

'Oops,' I said. 'Wait, hang on.'

I fixed it.

'There!' I said. 'That's how we write. When Dad makes a book about you, you'll need to sign it for people in bookshops. So you might as well learn how to do it now.' I gave Perijee the stick. 'You try.'

He took the stick and carved something into the bog beside me. Two vertical lines, criss-crossed like teeth. I frowned.

'That's not a word,' I said.

Perijee pointed to his chest – the same symbol was carved there, just below his shoulder.

'*Perijee*,' he said.

I shook my head. 'No – that's not English. It's not even French.'

Perijee looked confused. He pointed to another symbol on his neck. '... *Perijee*?'

I shook my head. 'I don't know *what* that is. It

looks like a Z, covered in tentacles. Don't *you* know what any of those . . . *things* mean?'

Perijee looked down at his body. Suddenly his smile disappeared – like it had been rubbed out. He sprouted fingers and ran them all over his body, tracing the carvings over and over and whining. I put my hand on his shoulder.

'Hey!' I said. 'Don't worry – we've got loads of time to work out what they say. Dad'll help you translate them when he gets back – promise.'

Perijee's smile popped back up, like a balloon on a string. He pointed to the sky.

'Clouds!' he said.

I smiled. 'Well remembered, Perijee! *Clouds.*'

A dot of rain hit my face.

'Oh,' I said. 'Right.'

By the time we got back, the bathtub was already half full of murky water. Perijee jumped inside and splashed around, squeaking with delight. I pulled him out.

'No!' I cried. 'You can't sleep in there! You'll catch a cold! How the hell is it *still* raining?' I shook my fist at the clouds. '*Stupid fake summer!*'

'food,' said Perijee, pulling my leg.

I ignored him and looked around the field in the hammering rain. There was nowhere for him to hide – not even any shelter.

'You'll have to sleep under a bush or something,' I said. 'If Mum sees you now ...'

'food,' said Perijee, yanking my leg harder.

'No!' I said. 'There *is* no more food! Don't you get it? You've eaten everything on this flipping island!'

'foooood,' said Perijee, chewing the taps off the bathtub.

I put my head in my hands. It was no good – the more Perijee ate, the more he seemed to want. He'd already grown another inch since morning. I couldn't look after him for the next six weeks by myself – I needed help, and lots of it.

But who was there around here with *that* much free time?

'Frank!'

He was bang on time for our first meeting. I was going to add 'you look nice today', but he didn't. He looked like a man who'd woken up at five in the morning and didn't like it. He smacked the boat against the jetty and staggered ashore.

'Coffee,' he said. 'Now.'

'Time for all that later!' I said. 'First, I have something to show you.'

I walked to the hut at the end of the jetty and opened the door. Frank rubbed his face.

'What's in there?' he muttered.

'Just look,' I said.

Frank thought about saying something, then changed his mind. He slumped into the hut.

Thinking about it, I should have given him some warning first. I don't know what he *was* expecting to see, but it probably wasn't Perijee covered in blood and ripping the head off a swordfish.

'Goodness gracious me,' Frank exclaimed. 'What on earth is that strange creature?'

(Those weren't the exact words that Frank used, but he made me promise never to repeat the ones he actually said.)

'Frank, this is Perijee,' I said. 'He's a very hungry alien. Perijee, this is Frank. He lives on his own and has a glass eye.'

Frank and Perijee looked at each other.

'Aaaaaaaargh,' screamed Frank.

'Aaaaaaaargh,' screamed Perijee.

Frank grabbed an oar and charged at Perijee like a madman. Perijee leapt ten feet into the air.

'Frank – no!' I cried. 'What are you doing?'

'Get back, Caitlin!' he shouted.

Frank waved the oar like a battleaxe while Perijee clung on to the ceiling above him and hissed. His body was slowly turning purple.

'Frank, stop it!' I cried. 'You're frightening him!'

Perijee was turning more purple by the second – and that wasn't all he was doing. He was swelling up like a balloon, stretching against the ceiling and splintering the rafters. It was like something horrible was growing out of him and he couldn't stop it. I had to do something, quick.

'Perijee, look!'

I ran up to Frank and gave him a big hug.

'See, Perijee? He's a *friend*! He won't hurt you!'

Perijee stopped growing. He stayed the same bigger size though, his eyes fixed on the oar in Frank's hands.

'Put the oar down,' I whispered.

'No,' Frank whispered back.

'He thinks you're trying to hurt him.'

'I am trying to hurt him.'

'*Frank.*'

He saw how serious I was and dropped the oar. The second he did, Perijee's chest sank like a balloon and his body turned back to white. Soon he was his old size again. He dropped down from the ceiling and hid between my legs, peeking out at Frank. I beamed.

'Great, isn't he?' I said. 'I think he fell from a meteor. Anyway, I'm teaching him maths.'

Frank didn't say anything for a while. He just stood with his mouth hanging open like a big beardy fish.

'Caitlin,' he said quietly. 'Get out the hut right now

and run back home as fast as you can.'

I blinked. 'Er . . . OK. Should I take Perijee with me?'

Frank glared at me. 'No!'

'Why not?' I said.

'*Because he's a flipping alien covered in blood!*'

'It's not human blood,' I said.

Frank looked like he was trying really hard not to start crying.

'Caitlin – listen to me,' he said. 'This thing, this – *Perijee*, whatever you're calling it – is not some pet. It is very dangerous. I don't think you understand *quite* how dangerous it is . . .'

'Oh Frank, *please*,' I said, rolling my eyes. 'Perijee – who is a *he*, by the way, not an *it* – is completely safe. The swordfish was dead already – we found it in a tree! And I've taught him not to kill things. I'm making sure he knows everything about living on Earth before Dad gets back.'

Frank almost choked.

'Your dad?!' he said. 'Caitlin – for the love of god, this is something for the army to deal with, not your flipping *dad* . . . !'

'Why not?' I said. 'Dad knows more about aliens than anyone in the world! Besides, if we tell the army they might attack him. They might think he's a *monster.*'

'He is a monster!' Frank shouted. 'He just grew ten feet tall!!'

'Because he thought *you* were going to hurt him!' I shouted back.

Frank laughed. 'Well, what if it happens again one day? What if he gets confused and tries to attack you?'

Frank just didn't get things sometimes. I grabbed Perijee and twanged the bobble on his head.

'See that?' I said. 'It's supposed to be my hat. He grew it himself after I saved him from the bogs.'

Frank blinked. '. . . So?'

'*So,*' I said patiently, 'he made a choice. He doesn't want to be a prawn or a frog. He doesn't want to be an alien. He wants to be a *person*. And I have to help him do it.'

'Why?' said Frank.

I sighed and took Perijee's hand.

'*Because,*' I said, 'I'm his sister.'

Perijee looked at me, his smile drifting up between his eyes like a bubble.

'Cait-lin,' he said quietly.

His whole body started glowing. The markings

across his body stood out and burned like bulbs, until they were almost too bright to look at. The room lit up like a lantern around us. Frank's mouth fell open.

'Those ... symbols,' he murmured in disbelief. 'What the hell are they?'

'I don't know.' I sighed. 'Neither does he. But he *really* wants to find out what they mean. I think they're important – something that tells him where he came from, or what he's doing here.'

Perijee stopped glowing. I picked him up and hugged him, but it was hard work – he was pretty heavy now.

'Dad will know how to translate them,' I said. 'That's why we need to keep Perijee safe until he gets back.'

Frank frowned. 'Hang on – "we"?'

'You're going to help me,' I said.

Frank said lots more things that I'm not allowed to write down.

'Just to get some fish for him!' I explained. 'So he doesn't starve to death – like, maybe a boatload a day or something ...'

Frank wasn't listening because he was too busy running round in circles.

'No!' he said. 'I'm not doing it, Caitlin!'

I grabbed his hand. 'Frank – please. I need you to help me. You're my *friend* ...'

Frank's face softened, just for a second. Then he snatched his hand away.

'NO!' he shouted. 'Not this time, Caitlin – I don't care how much you guilt me or beg me, there is *nothing* you can say to make me change my mind! You hear me? NOTHING!'

'But ...'

'*No, no, no, no, NO!*'

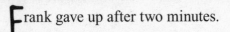

Frank gave up after two minutes.

The hut became Perijee's new home. Frank went out to catch fish every morning while Perijee and me wandered round the island, learning new words. Then at night Frank would haul back his catch to the beach for Perijee to eat. He became a pretty good fisherman. I think he even started to like Perijee.

'I hate that little weirdo,' said Frank.

'You're still helping him,' I said.

'I'm not doing it for him,' Frank muttered.

We watched Perijee work his way through a pile of fish twice his size. He loved fish more than anything.

'He's getting bigger, you know,' said Frank. 'He'll be bigger than you soon.'

'I know!' I said excitedly. 'Then he can carry me!'

Frank coughed.

'Any idea when he's going to *stop* growing, sprat?'

Perijee was emptying a bucket of haddock into his mouth like it was a tube of Smarties.

'No,' I said. 'But he can't get *that* much bigger, can he?'

'This is a camera,' I said.

Perijee smelled it.

'It's called a Polaroid,' I said. 'It's an old man camera. That's why Frank has one. He said we should be "documenting your growth" rather than "larking about all day like a pair of morons".'

I found a big rock to balance the camera on and turned round. I jumped. Perijee was standing right behind me. He was almost as big as me now.

'Breakfast again please,' he said.

'No!' I said. 'This is important. Plus – what have I told you about following people? We don't want you to scare Dad like you scared Frank.'

I pressed the timer button.

'Quick!' I said. 'Smile at the camera. And do the peace sign with your fingers.'

We both did the peace sign. The camera snapped and spat out a picture. It was all black at first, but after a few seconds shapes and colours started appearing like they were coming up from dark water.

'There,' I said, holding up the photo. 'That's you and me, in the middle.'

It was a bit blurry and rubbish, but there we were, our arms around each other and the sun behind us. Perijee looked at it in amazement.

'Caitlin and Perijee,' he said. 'Friends. Family.'

I smiled. 'Yes! Well remembered, Perijee.'

He ran his fingers over the photo. His whole body started changing. He was green and then pink and then red and then blue all over, his skin speckling and dancing through colours.

'I didn't know you could do that,' I said.

Perijee just looked at the photo.

'Family,' he said quietly.

'This is the sea,' I said.

I stood up to my knees in the water. Perijee was walking back and forth along the beach, wearing my old swimsuit and arm bands. They were already too small for him.

'Come on!' I said. 'It's just ground, with water on top – see?' I stomped up and down. 'That's all the ocean is. Hills and valleys covered in water.

Middle Island's like the top of a big underwater mountain.'

Perijee stepped nervously into the sea.

'Cold and wet,' he said.

'Stop whining,' I said.

The deeper Perijee got, the more he seemed to like it. Soon he was doggy-paddling around me and chirruping like a happy cat.

'Hey!' I said. 'You're actually really good at this. Who knows – maybe there's water on Sirius, too.'

Perijee turned his hands into flippers and started swimming out ahead of me. I grabbed him before he went too far.

'Careful!' I said. 'It gets deep, you know. *Really* deep. That's what Mum's job is – I mean, *was*. Exploring deep water. She used to work above the Mariana Trench.'

Perijee looked at me. 'Marry inner chench?'

'*Mariana Trench*,' I said. 'It's the deepest part of the sea. It goes down for seven whole miles. You could fit the whole of Mount Everest in there. There's not even any sunlight after the first half-mile down – just pitch black.'

Perijee held my hand.

'And it's filled with fish, too,' I said. 'Fish with

enormous eyes and see-through skin. Fish that look like spaceships.'

Perijee stepped a little closer to me.

'It's the most unexplored part of the whole world,' I said. 'There could be *anything* hiding down there – maybe even sea monsters! Who knows? But it just keeps going down, deeper and deeper ...'

Perijee started trying to climb on top of me.

'Hey!' I said. 'Get off! Come on, you're too big for that now!'

'Monsters,' said Perijee, growing extra legs and wrapping them round me.

After Frank left each night, Perijee and I would wander the beach until it was dark enough to see the stars. That's one nice thing about Middle Island. Back in the city, you'd be lucky to look up and see any stars at all. But out here the sky is so dark and so big, it's like looking into a whole other world.

We sat down on the shingle and I leaned against Perijee. He was bigger than me now.

'Sirius?' he said, pointing at a plane.

I moved his hand. 'Er ... over there, actually.'

Perijee gazed at the star. He started glowing, ever so faintly, lighting up the tiny bugs in the shingle.

'Home,' he said.

I smiled. 'Frank told me sailors in olden days used the stars as a map. Sirius always leads the way to the south. You could even use it to find your way home, if you knew which star it was.'

I lay on my back. I thought how good it would be to have a map in the sky, one that showed you how to get to wherever you wanted.

'Maybe *that's* what the symbols on your body are,' I said. 'They're not letters or numbers – they're a map. Telling you where you come from and how to get back again.'

There was silence for a moment. The waves came in, and out.

'Perijee,' I said. 'Do you think much about where you came from?'

Perijee didn't say anything.

'Perijee?'

I sat up. He wasn't beside me any more. He was in the sea. His arms were stretched out ahead of him and he was getting deeper with every step, his head sinking down and down . . .

'*Perijee, no!*' I cried.

A big wave appeared out of nowhere and knocked him backwards. The shock of it terrified him and he started splashing about, spluttering for breath. I didn't even have time to take off my clothes. I charged straight into the sea and got to him just in time, dragging him back to shore and throwing him onto the shingle.

'*What were you thinking?*' I shouted.

Perijee lay on his front, coughing up water.

'H-home,' he spluttered.

I didn't understand at first – but then I turned to the sea. The whole night sky was reflected on the water ahead of us, like a giant mirror. And right in the middle was Sirius.

'. . . You thought you could swim there?' I said. 'To space?'

I laughed, but it wasn't real laughter. I didn't feel happy.

'You . . . you were just going to *leave*?'

I clenched my fists. I was almost shaking – I thought I was going to walk off, or worse. But I didn't. I sat down on the shingle and said nothing.

It was silent for a while, except for the wind over the island. I felt a wet body huddle up against mine. Perijee peered into my face.

'Caitlin,' he said. 'I am sorr—'

He stopped, because I was crying. He didn't

understand what it was – he'd never seen tears before. He took off my hat and started trying to rub my face dry. I held his hand there, his fingers glowing and fading through the wool.

'You can't go, Perijee,' I said quietly. 'You're my *friend*. We're supposed to look after each other – no matter what.'

I held him and looked into his eyes. I *had* to make him understand.

'You're the reason Dad's going to come back,' I said. 'When he discovers you, he'll be the most famous scientist in the world. He won't have to do the tours any more. Him and Mum won't argue all the time ... it'll be just like it was before. We'll be able to do things together – go sailing, or go to the theatre ...'

'family,' said Perijee.

'Exactly, Perijee! A *family*!' I said. 'And you can be part of it! You've got everything you need here – food, a bed ... I mean, what more do you *want*?'

Perijee looked up at the stars.

'Home,' he said.

I frowned. 'But *this* is your home, Perijee! Here with me ...'

I turned to him, huddled on the stones – and

stopped. He looked so strange, and so lost – and so alone. Suddenly it was like I was seeing him for the first time. He would *always* be lost – no matter where he went on Earth.

'Oh, Perijee,' I whispered. 'I ... I'm sorry, I never ...'

I was so ashamed. I had never once thought about what he wanted. I had never even *asked*.

... What kind of friend did that?

I held his head in my hands.

'I'll get you home, Perijee. I promise. When Dad gets back ... we'll find a way.'

Perijee glowed.

'Promise?' he said.

I held him tight. 'Promise.'

The two of us sat huddled under a map of stars, while the moon grew closer and closer.

Dad's car was in the driveway.

I stood staring at it in shock. It shouldn't have been there. Dad wasn't supposed to be back for *weeks*. But there it was.

I looked at the house. The front door was open. The kitchen light was on. He was inside, waiting for me.

My dad.

I'd only just put Perijee to bed. I ran to the hut to get him and dragged him back across the island, cramming him into the woodshed.

'This is it!' I hissed, my heart thumping. 'Everything we've been working for – you ready?'

Perijee shook his head.

'Sure you are!' I said. 'The plan, remember?'

I gave him the egg timer and turned the dial till it clicked.

'Ten minutes,' I said, pointing at the numbers. 'When it rings, you come into the kitchen. I'll be there with Mum and Dad. Remember – don't move too fast or you might scare them. I'll introduce you. You walk up to Dad, shake his hand and say, "I loved your book."'

'I-I loved your book,' said Perijee, his voice shaking.

He turned purple. I squeezed his hand.

'Hey – don't be frightened,' I said. 'This is how we're going to get you home. Dad's been talking about aliens ever since I can remember. You're what he's been waiting for his whole life.'

Perijee's skin rippled.

'Trust me,' I said with a smile. 'He's going to love you.'

The door to the kitchen was shut. I waited for a moment in the corridor. My heart was beating like crazy. I always get like that when Dad comes back.

I could hear him and Mum talking inside. They were whispering.

They must want to surprise me, I thought.

I knocked. The whispering stopped right away.

'Come in,' said a voice. The same one I heard

down the phone once a month, square and sensible like a briefcase.

I opened the door and stepped inside. Mum was sat at the kitchen table. On the other side of the table was Dad.

It was strange, seeing him right in front of me instead of on one of his books. My chest went all tight and I didn't know what to say.

Then I remembered the plan. I clapped my hands to my face.

'Why . . . *Dad!*' I gasped. 'I thought you weren't back till September!'

Dad glanced at Mum.

'Er . . . no,' he said. 'I wasn't meant to be.'

He didn't say anything else. It was weird. It wasn't like the surprises you see in films – it was like him and Mum had just had another argument. I cleared my throat.

'Well,' I said. 'You've come at the perfect time! I have something *very* exciting to show you. But before I do, I should warn you both that . . .'

'Caitlin,' said Mum.

Her face was dead serious. She pulled out a chair.

'Sit down, darling,' she said. 'We need to talk.'

I was annoyed at first. Why was she trying to spoil my big moment? Why was she always . . .

And then I looked down at the table and saw the brown envelope with the school logo on the front.

My report!

I'd been so busy with Perijee that I'd completely forgotten about it. Now Mum knew the truth . . . and she must have called Dad back. I had to clear this up, quick.

'Mum – Dad,' I said. 'I'm really sorry. I should have told you both the truth ages ago. But if you just let me show you something, you'll see that . . .'

'Told us what?' said Mum, confused. 'What are you talking about, Caitlin?'

I pointed at the envelope. 'My . . . my school report.'

Mum pushed the envelope to one side. It hadn't even been opened. Dad scraped out the chair even further.

'Just sit down,' he said.

I sat down. The room around me filled with heavy silence. The type you get when something is really wrong.

'What's going on?' I said.

Mum took my hand.

'Caitlin,' she said. 'I'm worried about you.'

She was trying to hide things with her voice. Like broken glass at the bottom of a lake.

'I worry you're not happy,' she said. 'You talk about your friends at school, but I never see them. You keep bringing animals home. And the stories you make up . . . I worry that moving up here was a mistake for you. I worry that you're *lonely.*'

I blinked. She was right. I *had* been lonely . . . but not any more. Not now I had Perijee.

'I . . .' I began.

'Your mother and I aren't happy, either,' said Dad, cutting me off. 'We thought we could start a new life up here – make it work somehow. We thought the move would change things. But we were wrong.'

It was like he was talking about something else. He wasn't even looking at me.

'We can't fix something that broke a long time ago,' he said bitterly.

The whole room was changing around me. It was like a big black curtain was dropping from the ceiling and no one was stopping it. Suddenly I was really frightened and I didn't know why. Mum squeezed my hand.

'Do you understand what we're saying, Caitlin?'

I shook my head. 'N-no, I . . .'

'For crying out loud, Emily, just say it,' said Dad. 'There's no point trying to be clever with her.'

Mum glared at him. She turned to me and took a deep breath.

'Caitlin,' she said, 'your father's not going to come back from the book tour.'

I felt like my legs had been kicked out from under me.

'He's moving back to the city,' said Mum. 'You and I are going to stay here.'

My head spun. 'But – but why . . .'

'We're getting a divorce.'

RRRRIIIIIIIIIIIINNNNNNNGGGGGGGGG.

The sound made all three of us jump. Dad stood up.

'What the hell was that?' he said.

It was coming from behind the kitchen door. My heart dropped.

'Oh n—'

The door burst open and Perijee charged inside, the ringing egg timer clutched in his hand. The second I saw him I realised what he actually looked like – that he was too big for the house, much too big, so big that he smashed his head against the pans hanging from the ceiling and sent a stack of plates crashing to the floor. He roared in pain and the sound filled the room like an explosion.

Everything happened at once. Mum and Dad leapt up and threw themselves against the wall. Perijee saw Dad and stumbled towards him.

'I . . . I . . .' he croaked.

It looked wrong, all wrong. He looked like a monster. Suddenly Dad was reaching for the poker and swinging it at him . . .

'*Dad, no!*' I cried.

I was too late. The poker struck Perijee across the face like a thundercrack, and he reeled back and slipped on the plates and hit the ground, head first.

Everything stopped as quickly as it started. The pans were still ringing on their hooks.

'Oh my god,' said Mum.

For some reason I couldn't move. I was glued to the spot, just staring at the body on the floor. Perijee wasn't moving either. I should have run to him, tried to help him . . . but I couldn't. I couldn't do *anything*.

'It's dead,' said Dad.

And that was too much.

'He's not an *it*,' I choked. 'He's not an . . . *IT!*'

I threw myself at Perijee, but Mum grabbed me and held me back.

'Caitlin, what are you ...'

'He was just trying to say *hello*!' I cried. 'I told him you'd help him, that you'd get him back home, and now *look* at what you've done, look at him, he's—'

I turned round and the words stopped.

Perijee was standing up in front of us.

There was a dent in his head where the poker had hit him. One of his eyes had been knocked down his face and was hanging off his chin like a raindrop. He looked at us sheepishly.

Then, slowly – like a lava lamp – his face shifted back into place.

Dad dropped the poker.

Perijee kept changing. The dent in his head knocked out with a *pop*. His eye sucked back up like nothing had happened. He turned to Dad and coughed.

'I loved your book,' he said.

I broke away from Mum and threw my arms round him so tight I thought I really would kill him this time.

'Oh, Perijee!' I cried. 'I'm so so sorry, I never thought ...'

'GET AWAY FROM HER.'

Mum was right behind us, her eyes fixed on Perijee, her whole body curled up like a cat. I tried to block her.

'No, Mum – he's not dangerous! He—'

'Paul,' said Mum, holding out her hand. 'Give me the poker.'

Dad didn't answer. Mum glanced sideways.

'Paul,' she said. 'The . . .'

She trailed off. Dad was staring at Perijee. I'd never seen the look on his face before. He'd taken off his glasses.

'He talked,' said Dad. 'In English. He spoke to me.'

Mum looked at him nervously. '. . . Paul? Paul, what are you doing?'

Dad took a step towards us. Perijee cried out and hid behind me, shaking with fear. Dad looked at me with pleading eyes.

'Please,' he begged. 'Tell him I'm not going to hurt him.'

Mum gasped. *'Paul . . . !'*

It was the first time Dad had ever asked me for anything. My whole body flooded with a thousand different feelings, like Perijee changing colours.

'It's OK,' I said, crouching down to Perijee. 'Dad wants to help.' I held out my hand. 'You trust me – don't you?'

Perijee took my hand and we stood up. Dad walked towards us, slow and careful, like the floor was made of the most beautiful flowers. Then he and Perijee stood facing each other. They were almost the same height.

'Those . . . those markings,' Dad whispered.

I leaned forwards, trying to get between them.

'He's always had them,' I said. 'Even when I found him, just after the meteor shower. He was only the size of a prawn back then.'

Dad's face drained. '. . . He's grown that fast?'

'He learns fast, too!' I said. 'I'm the one who taught him how to speak.' I swallowed. 'I – I called him Perijee. I got it from one of your books . . .'

Dad stumbled away from me, a hand on his head.

'I have to get everyone here,' he said. 'Right now.'

He pulled his phone out his pocket and started dialling. I grabbed his arm.

'*No!*' I shouted. 'You can't!'

Dad stared at me in shock. 'Caitlin, what are . . .'

'You can't tell anyone about him!' I explained.

'They'll take him away! I promised you'd get him back home!'

Dad laughed and pulled away. 'Caitlin, come on – this may be the most important discovery in history, I *have* to—'

'No you don't,' I said, desperate. 'You can study him here by yourself. He's your discovery – no one else's. I ... I'll show you everything I know about him. We'll do it together – just the two of us.'

Dad said nothing. I clutched his arm.

'Please,' I begged. 'Please don't take him away from me.'

I could see Dad trying to work something out, right at the back of his eyes. Then he put away his phone.

'Fine,' he said quietly. 'I won't tell anyone. I'll have to go back to the mainland though – to pick up some equipment. I'll be back tomorrow morning.'

'*You WHAT?!*'

We spun round. Mum was holding on to a chair for support.

'Have you gone *mad*?' she cried. '*You can't keep an alien in the house with your DAUGHTER!*'

'We don't have a choice,' said Dad, his voice hard and cold. 'Caitlin's right. I'll need a few weeks to study him before deciding on the best course of action – that's all.'

Mum was beside herself. *'A few WEEKS ... ?'*

Dad didn't listen to a word she said. He grabbed his briefcase and marched out the door. Just before he left, he turned back to face me. He was smiling. My heart glowed.

Then I realised that he was looking at Perijee.

'Beautiful,' he whispered.

There was the sound of car wheels speeding across gravel, and then nothing.

Me and Mum were left standing in the kitchen. We seemed miles apart somehow. Perijee stood between us, his head nearly touching the ceiling.

'The animal in the guest room.' Mum sighed. 'It was him, wasn't it?'

I shuffled my feet. 'I did try to tell you.'

When I looked up, Mum wasn't looking at Perijee. She was looking at me, like I was the one covered in letters that made no sense.

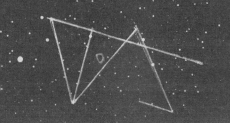

I walked into the kitchen the next morning and Mum was fast asleep on a chair. We hadn't talked much after Dad left – I'd wanted to celebrate the fact he was coming back, but Mum was refusing to see the positive side. She didn't even want Perijee in the house. I think she was afraid of him. That was probably why she was holding a pickaxe.

'Mum?' I said.

She jerked upright, her eyes wide open.

'Jesus!' She clutched her chest. 'Don't walk in on me like that, Caitlin! I thought you were ...'

Perijee walked in behind me – he'd spent the night curled up on my beanbag. Mum flew to her feet and the two of them faced each other across the room, bristling. I shuffled nervously.

'Er ... pancakes, anyone?'

I strolled over to the oven, humming merrily. *So*

long as I act like nothing is weird, I thought, *then it will all be fine.*

I hit the oven with the poker until it worked, then turned back round. Perijee was sniffing the spice cupboard and Mum was slowly creeping towards the knife rack.

'Mum?' I said. 'Pancakes?'

She swung round, her face tight. 'Yes! Pancakes! Lovely!'

I grinned. 'Great! What about you, Perijee?'

He didn't answer. He was completely still, staring at a wall. He was changing. His eyes had become big and blurry, flashing between colours. His skin twitched and flickered like hair in the wind.

Then, just like that, he stopped.

'Seventeen,' he said.

I didn't even know he could count that high.

'. . . You want seventeen pancakes?' I said. I looked at the cupboard. 'I don't know if we have enough butter . . .'

All the doors were kicked in and the next thing I knew seventeen soldiers with gas masks and rifles were stood in a circle around us.

'*GET HER OUT OF HERE!*' bellowed one, pointing at me.

Before I knew what was happening Mum had thrown me over her shoulder and was running outside. The last thing I saw was Perijee, his face a mask of fear as the ring of soldiers closed around him. His body was already starting to grow.

'*Perijee, no!*' I cried.

The whole island was swarming in helicopters. The house was surrounded by barbed wire. Everywhere I looked there were soldiers aiming rifles at the kitchen.

'What are they doing here?' I said. 'Mum, what's happening?'

Mum just kept running. Through the kitchen windows behind us I could make out flashes of light, bodies being thrown around like rag dolls. I could see Perijee's arms flailing in the smoke.

'*Mum, they're hurting him!*' I cried. '*Make them stop!*'

Suddenly soldiers were racing out the kitchen door, smoke pouring out behind them. Something inside the house was screaming. It wasn't a human scream. It was growing louder and louder, until soon it was so loud that it shook the ground and made the air tremble. I hammered at Mum's back.

'*Let me go!*' I shouted. '*I have to get back to him before . . .*'

BOOM.

The house burst apart in a cloud of bricks and dust. We hit the ground. Eight giant tentacles were crawling out the smoke, each one thick as a tree trunk, heaving Perijee into the daylight like a bird from a shell.

Only he wasn't Perijee any more. He was a hundred feet tall, covered in eyes and teeth and tentacles. I leapt to my feet.

'*Perijee, don't be afraid!*' I cried. '*I'm right here! I—*'

The army all attacked him at once. Perijee screamed with fear and charged across the garden, smashing helicopters out the air and scattering the soldiers around him like flies. In one great leap he flew over the trees and came crashing down into the cove, crushing the jetty into splinters and hitting the water like a bomb going off.

And just like that, he was gone.

The garden was silent. The tower of water he had sent up behind him disappeared. Seaspray fell around us like rain.

'Caitlin,' Mum was shouting. 'Caitlin, are you all right? *Caitlin!*'

I didn't answer her. I was watching Perijee's

enormous shadow disappear from the island like a torpedo. A great white wave was rising up above him, growing bigger and faster with every second.

It was heading towards the mainland.

They put me and Mum in a helicopter with two soldiers.

I sat in silence with a blanket around me. I had no idea what was going on – every time I tried to work out what had just happened, none of it made any sense. All I knew was that Perijee had gone.

A TV in the back of the helicopter was showing the news. You could see the towns that had already been destroyed on the mainland, and people being evacuated from their homes all over the country, and soldiers herding people into enormous shelters. Mum just sat there, shaking her head.

'It's like the end of the world,' she whispered.

Suddenly the report switched to a man at a desk.

'We interrupt this broadcast with breaking news,' he said. 'The alien invader has just launched an attack on our capital city.'

Everyone gasped. The camera cut away and when it came into focus all you could see was a sky filled with smoke.

Below it lay the city – or what was left of it. There was a river, and what used to be a bridge, and that was it. Everything else was on fire.

Somewhere through the smoke you could make out a huge body snaking up from the water, so large it crushed whole streets beneath it, and a giant head roaring with anger.

I could have cried.

'Oh, Perijee,' I whispered.

He was a monster now. There was nothing left of him that I could recognise. Nothing of the sweet, loving alien I'd known. The one I'd taught to read, the one that I'd shown the stars to . . . he was gone.

. . . And then I saw him.

'Miss,' the soldier next to me said, 'you can't stand up in the helicopter.'

I didn't listen. I pressed myself up against the TV, my hands shaking.

'Miss, please sit down.'

There, right on top of the monster's head – so

small you could easily miss it – something was sticking out. Like a fin or an antenna.

Or a person.

A person wearing a bobble hat.

'It's him!' I cried. *'It's Perijee, there at the top, look ... !'*

The soldiers were already dragging me back to my chair. Mum was screaming at them to let me go. I didn't care. I just kept staring at the screen and laughing.

There was Perijee, right on top of the monster's head. It wasn't really him doing all those terrible things – it was something else, something that had grown out of him when he was so frightened that he had no other choice. But deep down he was still there ... still alive. Still Perijee.

I turned to Mum, my eyes shining with tears.

'He's wearing my hat!'

The way the camp worked was like this:

1. It wasn't like a real camp. Real camps have tents and campfires. This was just a massive room with hundreds of beds separated by sheets on bits of wire. Kind of like a giant sleepover, but with guards at the door who shot you if you tried to leave.

2. The camp was for keeping people safe. There were camps all over the country, and everyone had to live in them until the army got 'The Monster' under control. That's what they called the thing that grew out of Perijee. There were other names for him too, much worse ones than that, but I can't tell you what they were.

3. There were loads of rules. You had to stay in bed after lights out. You couldn't leave the room, ever. Some people tried to escape because they wanted to go home, but the guards always caught them.

4. You only got to use the showers once a day, which was a pity because they were *amazing*! The doors were sealed all around the edges, so if you plugged the drain up with towels and left the water running for about half an hour the cubicle became a big hot bath you could stand up in, or a tropical whirlpool if you ran around in circles. You had to do it early though because some IDIOT kept using up all the hot water.

5. There was nothing else to do except sit around all day. They played the news once in the morning and once in the evening, and that was it. The rest of the time you were left alone with your thoughts.

6. I thought about Perijee. Obviously.

'... Caitlin?'

I'd been awake for hours. Mum sat up in the bed

opposite, rubbing her eyes. When the helicopter had dropped us at the camp a week before, they'd made sure that the two of us had our own cubicle. Mum said not all families were so lucky – there were people I knew from school who were sleeping on the floor by the toilets. But I still didn't feel that lucky.

'I'm amazed *anyone* can sleep in this place,' said Mum. 'Not exactly the Hilton, is it?'

She smiled at me.

'Hey – maybe when we get out of here, I'll treat us to a night in the *real* Hilton. Just the two of us. That'd be nice, wouldn't it?'

I said nothing. Mum's face fell.

'Caitlin,' she said. 'Please. I know you're upset, but you can't just stop *talking* to me . . .'

She'd said it all a hundred times before, ever since we first got here. I could say it along with her word for word. Especially the next bit.

'*I had to do it!*'

She held out her arms to the room around her.

'I mean, just look at what it's done in seven days! It's torn the country apart! Your father was out of his mind, suggesting we keep it at home in the first place . . . Can you imagine what might have happened if I *hadn't* phoned the police?'

I stared at Mum in disgust. She was the reason the army had shown up. The reason Perijee had been attacked. The reason the Monster had grown out of him and carried him away. The reason we were now stuck inside the camp, with no idea where Dad was.

Dad.

He'd agreed to help Perijee. The two of us were going to do it together – find out where he came from, get him home. But it was all ruined now. He had no idea where I was. He was probably wandering the country right now, trying to find me. And it was all Mum's fault.

'I'm going to watch the news,' I said.

I left before she could say anything else.

There was a massive crowd around the TV, as usual, watching in silence. I pushed my way to the front. Onscreen was the city. The river had burst its banks days ago and all the streets were under water. It looked like an ocean now, dotted with broken buildings and shattered planes.

And right in the middle of it, like a huge white island ...

'Look at him,' someone in the crowd muttered

beside me. 'I could swear he's grown bigger since yesterday.'

The Monster was huge. His mouth rose out the water like an ancient cavern, fifty rows of teeth fading into darkness. His body stretched so far into the distance the cameras couldn't pick him up any more. You could just about make out the strange symbols carved into his sides that no one could understand, and the marks where bullets had hit him and done no damage at all.

And if you looked hard enough – though no one ever did – you could see a little white dot, right at the top of his head.

'Perijee,' I whispered.

Mum had made me promise not to tell anyone about what had happened – she said it wasn't safe. I hadn't breathed a word, of course, but not because she'd asked me. Because that was just the way I wanted it. Perijee was my secret – no one else's.

'An absolute *disgrace*!'

A woman shoved her way to the front of the crowd. I recognised her from back on the mainland – she'd got footballs banned from the school playground because they kept landing in her ornamental pond and upsetting the fish.

'Look at those so-called "warships"!' she spat. 'An alien invader's sitting right in front of them, and what do they do? *Nothing!*'

She jabbed a finger at the TV. A blockade of boats circled the Monster's head like a ring of toys. They were all tied together with chains to stop anyone from going near him.

'A few pathetic attempts to attack him, then they give up!' she cried. 'And they expect us to just sit here and wait ... We won't have any homes to go back to at this rate!'

The crowd cheered. The woman was getting more and more fired up.

'Well, I'm sick of waiting!' she screeched. 'If the army's not going to do anything about him, it's time *we* did! It's time we ...'

She glanced at the guards beside her. They were too busy pushing the crowds back from the TV to take any notice of her. She drew everyone around her into a tight huddle. I pushed my way in – not because I was interested in what she had to say, but because in camp you took any gossip you could get.

'It's time we *took action*,' said the woman in a hushed voice. 'We've all seen the footage of towns and cities on the news – there are still *thousands* of people on the outside! The army's too busy dealing with the Monster to try and force them into camps any more. There's even rumours of . . .'

She leaned forwards to whisper, and everyone huddled closer.

'Rumours of people . . . *coming together*,' she hissed. 'Taking charge for themselves. There's a big meeting in a town called Wanderly planned for the day after tomorrow – it's a hundred miles south of here. Everyone from the mainland is going to be there – they're going to fix this whole mess!'

Everyone in the crowd started muttering in excitement. The woman glanced round at them, her eyes flashing.

'I say we join them,' she said. 'I say we break out of here and get to Wanderly before it's too late . . . before there's nothing left to save!'

It was like someone had lit a fuse in the room. Everyone started talking all at once. For the first time in days, people looked happy – like they had hope again. And I knew exactly how they felt. Finally, things were going to go back to normal! I could get out of here and find Dad, and then together we could get Perijee back home and . . .

'That's right!' said the woman. 'Who needs the

army? We'll destroy the Monster ourselves!'

My heart almost stopped.

'*NOOO!*'

Everyone turned to look at me.

'You can't kill the Monster!' I said. 'You'll kill Perijee, too!'

This was met with a sea of blank faces.

'. . . Peri-what?' said the woman.

I almost stopped myself – but I had to tell them. This was too important.

'He's an alien that's living on top of the Monster,' I explained. 'You don't know him, but he's good, honest! He . . .'

'That's enough,' said a voice.

A dinnerlady was pushing through the crowd towards us. She had a big frilly hairnet on her head, and a smaller one over her beard.

'Frank!' I cried.

Everyone in camp had to have a job – it was supposed to stop people from worrying too much about the Monster. It worked! The day Frank got made a dinnerlady everyone stopped complaining about the end of the world and started complaining about how disgusting his food was instead.

'Tell them, Frank!' I said, dragging him closer. 'Tell them about Perijee!'

Frank looked at the crowd. He smiled and patted me on the head.

'Er . . . I think that's enough silly stories about the Monster, little girl,' he said.

My face fell. 'What? Frank, what are you . . .'

'Sounds like she's delirious.' Frank sighed, grabbing me by the wrist. 'I'd better take her to the medical room right away. Must have been something she ate.'

'Like your spam crumble,' another muttered.

'Or that milk you set on fire,' someone added.

Frank dragged me away. I kicked and shouted and fought against him, but it was no good – he kept pulling until the crowd was far behind us, and then swung round.

'*What are you playing at?*' he hissed. 'Telling people you knew him – that *I* knew him? Are you *insane*?'

'But Frank, they . . .'

'Look at them, Caitlin!'

He pointed at the crowd. A fight had broken out around the TV – not that it was a surprise. It happened almost every day. The guards were shoving everyone back, barking orders, trying to get them to calm down and only making it worse.

'People in here are just about ready to kill each other,' said Frank. 'Outside it's even worse. People living like savages, stealing whatever they can get their hands on ... The whole country's falling apart. There's even talk of mad cults wandering the countryside, saying the Monster's some kind of god – kidnapping people, Caitlin!' He looked me square in the eye. 'You start talking about Perijee now and you're going to get yourself hurt – or worse.'

I shook my head. 'But Frank ... didn't you hear what they said? They want to *kill* him!'

Frank placed a hand on my shoulder.

'Listen to me, sprat,' he said carefully. 'That thing – that *Perijee* – he's not what you remember. He's destroying the world now. And if someone doesn't stop him ...'

I grabbed him by the apron.

'But it's not *him* doing it, Frank! Remember when you scared him in the hut and he started growing? It's the same thing! The Monster must be something that grows out of him when he's being attacked – to protect him! He's *frightened*, Frank! We have to help him!'

'Caitlin ...'

'We need to get to this meeting in Wanderly,' I said. 'Then we can tell everyone about him – how frightened he is, and how it's not his fault, and then they'll *have* to listen and ...'

'Caitlin,' said Frank sadly. 'Do you really think they'll listen to anything you say?'

He pointed back to the crowd. The shouting and pushing was even worse now. None of them wanted to fix anything or make it better. They just wanted to fight.

'It's no good, sprat,' said Frank. 'There's nothing you can do. You ... you just have to forget about him.'

It almost knocked the breath out of me.

'Frank,' I said. 'You don't mean that.'

He sighed. 'Caitlin – if he's really as good as you say he is, then why is he still on top of that Monster, eh? Why isn't he trying to stop it?'

I didn't know what to say. I thought I could trust Frank more than anyone – but I was wrong. Frank shuffled his feet.

'I'm sorry,' he muttered, and left.

I turned back to the crowd. They were still fighting. The TV was wobbling and shaking on its stand, almost tipping over the edge, but no one was trying to stop it. No one was even watching the news any more – no one cared.

Which meant I was the only one who saw what was happening.

The cameras had zoomed to the top of the Monster's head.

Perijee was waving to the camera.

I gasped. It was the first time I'd been able to see him up close. There he was, still wearing the bobble hat and with his tiny dot eyes. But something was wrong – really wrong. He was sunk waist-deep into the Monster's head, trying to heave himself out. *That* was why he was still there – he was stuck. And he was shouting the same word, over and over . . .

Cait-lin.

He looked absolutely terrified. Just like when he was stuck in the mud.

And suddenly, I knew exactly what I had to do.

The lights had been turned off hours ago.

A single glimmer flickered in the bulb above my bed. It wasn't much, but there it was – a white dot in the darkness.

'I'm coming to get you, Perijee,' I whispered.

Frank had it all wrong. Just because people in camp wanted to hurt Perijee, it didn't mean that the rest of the world did. Once I'd shown everyone that Perijee was kind and gentle, they were *bound* to change their minds and listen to me. Then I could tell them my plan – how to save the world without hurting anyone.

But I couldn't just walk into the big meeting in Wanderly and say that Perijee was my friend. There was no *way* they'd believe me – not unless I had proof.

I reached under my mattress and pulled out the

photo. It was crinkled and battered from when I'd smuggled it into camp in my wellies, but you could still see Perijee and me in the middle, just about. We're standing on a beach, smiling to the camera, doing the peace sign. Perijee has his arm around me.

Because I was his friend. Because I saved him when he was stuck.

It was time to save him again.

I'd spent all day preparing my escape. First I stole a notebook out of a guard's pocket. All I wanted was a map of the camp, but when I looked through it I realised I'd hit the jackpot – he'd written down the secret password, too! Now all I had to do was walk up to an exit, say it to the guard on duty, and they'd let me stroll right past ... so long as they didn't recognise me, of course.

I pulled on the disguise I'd spent all afternoon making in the toilets. I turned to the mirror and smiled. It was *perfect*. There was no way the guards would recognise me now. Mum wouldn't even recognise me.

Mum.

She was fast asleep, facing the wall. For one mad moment, I wanted to wake her up and tell her everything – about how I was going to escape, how I was going to find Dad, how we were going to get Perijee home and put everything back to normal.

But of course, I couldn't do any of that now. She'd just try to stop me – like always.

I left without looking back.

The exit was the other side of the hall. Even in the dark I could see the guard standing at the doors. I took a deep breath. My plan had to go perfectly – one mistake and it would all be over.

I checked and rechecked the password until I knew it off by heart. Then I adjusted my disguise, took another deep breath and walked towards the exit.

With every step, my heart beat faster and faster. It felt like hours until I was standing in front of the glaring guard.

'Hey!' he said. 'What are you doing out of bed?'

I swallowed. This was it – my one chance. No going back.

'*Beef – oven*,' I said.

The guard stared at me. I gave him a wink.

'*Beef oven*,' I said again. 'You know – the password. The one that lets me go past. Beef oven.'

The guard was silent for a very long time.

'Do you mean "Beethoven"?' he said eventually.

My mouth went dry.

'. . . What?'

'The password is "Beethoven",' the guard explained. 'As in the celebrated composer and pianist Ludwig van Beethoven. Not "beef oven". That just sounds like you found the password and misread it.'

I could feel the blood draining out of my face. It was times like this that I really wished I could read properly.

'Er . . . yeah, well . . .'

'Also – what are you wearing?' said the guard.

He'd spotted my disguise. I quickly cleared my throat.

'It's obvious, isn't it?' I said. 'I'm a chef! That's why I'm wearing this hairnet – and an apron that says "chef" on it.'

'You've spelled "chef" with an "s",' said the guard. 'And the "e" is the wrong way round.'

This was going very badly.

'Oh! How strange!' I said. 'I'll have to fix that sometime! Well, it's been lovely to chat, but if you don't mind I need to get to the kitchen right away . . .'

'In the middle of the night?' said the guard.

I started sweating. 'Yes! That's right! Because ...
because ...'

I racked my brains for a good reason. *Think,
Caitlin, think ... !*

'Because I left the oven on!' I cried. 'Yeah, that's
it – and *that's* why I said "beef oven"! I was thinking
about the beef I left in the oven earlier! Which is
going to burn unless I get there right away!'

I put my hands on my hips in triumph. It was
hands down my all-time greatest lie.

'So,' I said, 'can you let me past, please?'

The guard thought about it.

'No.'

My face fell. 'Why not?'

'Because you're obviously not a chef,' said
the guard. 'You're ten years old. Also I can see a
guard's notebook sticking out of your pocket, which
is probably the one that was reported stolen earlier
today. Stealing off a guard is a very serious crime,
you know, Caitlin.'

I jumped.

'How ... how do you know my name?!'

'It's written on your bobble hat,' said the guard.
'Which I can see through your hairnet.'

I really regretted putting labels on all my things to help teach Perijee.

'Er ... right,' I said. 'Well, I can explain all that ...'

'Oh, you'll be doing a lot of explaining,' said the guard. 'About why you chose to break the three most important rules of camp: getting out of bed after lights out, attempting to escape, impersonating a chef ...'

There was a sudden crash on the other side of the room. We both spun round. The guard's face fell.

'What's going on over there?' he shouted. 'Who's out of bed?'

Silence. Then another smash. The end of the room was filled with voices, shouting, footsteps.

'*Get back!*' someone cried out in the darkness. '*All of you, back ... !*'

The crashes and shouts and bangs were getting louder. Suddenly another guard ran out of the darkness.

'Sir!' she said. 'Come, quick! Some people broke through the north exit – they're all escaping!'

The guard's face drained.

'Sound an alarm! Get everyone we have on the north side! No one escapes!'

They raced into the darkness. Within seconds a siren was ringing out, and more guards were pouring through the exit beside me. Everyone was climbing out of their beds, demanding to know what was going on. Soon the room was filled with people shouting and pushing and throwing things.

Which is why no one noticed me standing beside the open exit.

'Oh,' I said. 'Well, that was easy.'

I threw away the notebook, pulled off my disguise and strolled out the door.

At first I was worried I'd get caught the second I stepped outside. But there weren't any guards left to catch me. I walked out the front gates, and I'd escaped! One step closer to Perijee. Now all I had to do was find Wanderly.

'Er . . .' I said, looking around.

The countryside was pitch black. There was a road in front of me, but it was empty. There weren't even any roadsigns. Frank would have known what to do, but . . .

I shook my head. I didn't need Frank any more – he'd let me down, just like Mum. I could do this on my own. All I needed was to find which way was south . . .

A light on the horizon suddenly caught my eye. I gasped.

'Sirius!'

There it was, right ahead of me – the brightest star in the sky. So long as I followed it, I'd end up going south.

I set off along the empty road. After a few hours, the star seemed to get bigger, which was confusing – stars don't normally do that. The more I walked, the more it looked like it was actually next to the road.

Eventually I worked out it was a supermarket.

It was silent and empty, glowing beside the road like a spaceship. It was one of those massive ones, with a car park and three floors and a restaurant and everything. Someone had left all the lights on. I wondered if there was some food left inside. I hadn't eaten all day – I'd been too busy making my costume.

I walked inside and wandered the aisles, but it was no use – all the shelves had been cleared ages ago. I found a big pack of superglue that was slightly dented and that was it. I groaned. There was no *way* I could eat superglue. If I was going to walk a hundred miles in two days, I'd at least need a bag of crisps . . .

I stopped. I was *sure* I'd just heard something.

'Hello?'

No answer. I listened carefully. There it was again – coming through a set of doors beside me. It sounded like a cow being pushed into a lift.

I walked through the doors. At the end of the corridor was another girl, a year or two older than me. She had straight dark hair that just touched her shoulders, and pale white skin with sharp black freckles.

She was trying to push a cow into a lift.

The girl gave a final heave and the cow squeezed inside with an angry moo. She sighed with relief, turned around . . . and froze.

'What are you doing?' she snapped.

I didn't really know how to answer that.

'What are *you* doing?' I asked back.

Suddenly there was a sound behind me. People – lots of people.

'Rats,' said the girl.

She ran down the corridor and grabbed me.

'You and I are best friends,' she said.

I was stunned – months of trying to make friends, and I'd finally done it. Who knew it could be so easy!

'OK!' I said. 'Sure!'

'Actually, forget that,' said the girl. 'We're sisters.'

I frowned. '. . . What?'

'And there's no cow here,' she added.

She pressed a button and the lift shut with a little *ding*. At that exact moment a giant mob burst through the doors behind me, led by a farmer with a shotgun and a lump on his head the size of a breakfast muffin.

'*That's her!*' he shouted, pointing at the girl. 'That's the one who stole my cow!'

The mob charged forwards, waving their fists. We were trapped – there was nowhere to run. But the girl barely even blinked.

'Cow?' she said innocently. 'What cow?'

The mob screeched to a halt in front of us.

'You know *exactly* what cow!' the farmer shouted. 'Come on – own up, you little thief! Where is it?'

The girl looked confused. 'I – I don't know what you're talking about.'

There was a *ding* on the floor above us, and the sound of lift doors opening.

'My sister and I have been here all night and we haven't seen any cow,' said the girl, turning to face me. 'Have we, Annabelle?'

Everyone turned to look at me. I panicked.

'Er . . .' I said.

'Lies!' the farmer shouted. 'Look at them – they're both in on it!' He jabbed a finger at the girl. 'I'd recognise that face anywhere – came to my house asking for a glass of milk, she did, then locked me in a cleaning cupboard and stole my cow!'

The girl gasped in horror. 'Oh *no*, sir! I would *never* do such a thing!'

I could hear a set of hooves walking down a corridor above us.

'My sister and I are no criminals!' she cried, grabbing me tight. 'Our only crime is love – love for our poor, sick mother! We've been wandering this supermarket for hours, searching for medicine that might help her ...'

She gripped my wrist.

'... *Isn't that right, Annabelle?*'

I nodded furiously. 'That's right! We're sisters!'

The lies were working. The mob were shaking their heads at the farmer in disgust. I could see the cow going down an escalator behind them.

'Well ... maybe I was wrong,' said the farmer. 'I guess it was pretty dark when it happened ...'

The girl's eyes lit up.

'Hang on! Now that you mention it, we did see another girl run through here a few minutes ago ... *Didn't we, Annabelle?*'

She crushed my hand.

'We're sisters!' I screamed.

'Yes,' said the girl, tapping her chin. 'It was ever

so strange. She was carrying a bale of hay. And a milking stool. She just ran through those doors over there . . .'

The mob didn't need telling twice – they charged straight through the doors, roaring and shaking their fists. By the time they'd worked out they were inside a big cleaning cupboard, the girl had taken a padlock out her pocket and snapped it round the doorhandles.

'Word of advice.' She tested the doors. 'Stay away from supermarkets. Nothing worth taking.'

'Huh?' I said.

'Try further up north,' she said. 'There's some old factories a couple of miles off the road. No money left – trust me, I've checked – but if you can be bothered to get the lead flashing off the roof, you'll make an absolute packet selling it down in Wanderly.'

By now the mob were hammering on the doors behind her.

'Speaking of which,' said the girl, rolling her eyes. 'I need to get there myself before this lot try to take their cow back.' She strolled off. 'Well, see you around.'

She marched down the corridor without looking back. I ran after her.

'Hang on,' I said. 'You know the way to Wanderly?'

The girl laughed. 'Oh, *please*. You can stop with the whole "naïve idiot" routine now. I've been doing this long enough to know another fraud when I see one. You're not going to trick me out of the cow, so don't even try.'

'Er ... no, I'm not interested in the cow.' I scratched my head. 'To be honest, I don't even understand why you'd *want* to steal a cow in the first ...'

The girl spun round and grabbed me.

'Listen, chum,' she said. 'Quit while you're ahead. The cow's mine – I stole it fair and square. I don't care how clever you newcomers think you are, I was doing this *years* before the Monster turned up, and I'll be doing it long after you've been caught. Understand?'

I didn't understand at all, but I thought it would be pretty stupid to do anything other than nod. The girl's face softened.

'Glad we cleared that up,' she said, letting me go. 'My name's Fi, by the way – you'll have heard of me. What about you? Got a name?'

I couldn't tell her my real name – call me suspicious, but there was something about Fi that didn't seem completely trustworthy. After all, Frank had said there were dangerous people on the outside . . .

Frank.

I pushed his face out of my mind.

'Sure – I got a name. It's, er . . . Queenie.' I looked around me. 'Queenie McCeiling.'

Fi stared at me.

'Your name is Queenie McCeiling.'

'Yup,' I said. 'Sure is.'

'Are you sure it's not Caitlin?'

I started.

'Hey! How did you . . .'

'It's written on your hat.'

Stupid flipping labels. I had to think up a good lie, fast.

'Er . . . no,' I said. 'That's my hat's name.'

Fi looked at me. She searched my face for ages, like she was trying to find me in one of those Where's Wally pictures.

'You're not a professional fraud, are you?' she said.

I considered lying some more.

'No,' I said.

Fi nodded. 'And you want to get to Wanderly because . . .'

I clammed up. This time I really *couldn't* tell her the truth. What if she was just like the people in camp – what if she wanted the Monster dead too? She might even try to stop me getting to the meeting, and then my one chance to save Perijee would be gone. It was no use – I had to keep him a secret until I was safe in Wanderly.

'Er . . . I hear there's a big sale on,' I said.

Fi raised an eyebrow.

'Look,' she said. 'You clearly don't have a clue what you're doing. If you try and get to Wanderly on your own, you're going to get yourself killed, at best. So here's the deal: because you're obviously harmless, and because I feel sorry for you, you can come with me . . . but only if you do everything I say. I'll take you as far as Wanderly.' She held out a hand. 'Deal?'

I looked at the girl in front of me. She was a total stranger. She was a thief. For all I knew, she was going to steal all my stuff the first chance she got.

But she *did* know the way to Wanderly. And if that meant being able to get to the meeting in time . . .

I shook her hand.

'Deal,' I said. 'My name's Caitlin. I haven't really named my hat.'

'Really,' said Fi.

'Yeah, that was a lie.'

Fi nodded. 'Caitlin?'

'Yes?'

'Get the cow.'

I found the cow beside the pastry counter and coaxed it into the back of an ice-cream van with a Mr Whippy. Fi hotwired the engine and in less than two minutes we were on the road to Wanderly.

'I've never stolen a car before,' I said. 'Won't the police try to stop us?'

'Probably not,' said Fi. 'There's only one police car left round here and I stole it yesterday.'

I fell asleep in the passenger seat. When I woke up the next morning, the sun was shining and I felt like a different person. Partly because I was another step closer to saving Perijee, but also because my hat and watch had gone.

'Hey!' I said, sitting up. 'My stuff! It's disappeared!'

'How strange,' said Fi, looking innocent. 'Well, I'm sure it'll turn up somewhere.'

I checked my pockets and sighed with relief. The photo of Perijee and me was still there.

'Looking for something?' said Fi suspiciously.

'No!' I needed to change the subject, fast. 'Er . . . how much further to Wanderly?'

'A couple more hours yet.' Fi sighed. 'In fact . . . mind if you drive the last bit? I could do with a break.'

'I can't drive,' I said.

Fi shrugged. 'You'll learn.'

She pulled onto the hard shoulder and shifted over.

'Come on, then,' she said, patting the seat. 'Your go.'

I was amazed. Mum or Dad would *never* have let me drive a car – they wouldn't even let me ride that bike I found in the canal once. But Fi . . . well, she was different.

'You know, Fi,' I said, 'I've never had a friend like you.'

Fi scowled. 'What the hell are you on about? We're not friends.'

I nodded. 'Yeah – it's too early for that, isn't it? I guess you're more like my pal. Or my buddy. What would you call me?'

'Lots of things,' muttered Fi. 'Just drive the car, please.'

'Sure!' I pulled on my seat belt. 'So – which button makes it go faster?'

We stood in front of the smoking wreck of the van.

'That bridge came out of nowhere,' I said.

'Quite,' said Fi.

I looked down the long and empty road.

'So ... how long till we get to Wanderly *now*?'

'Well, we won't be there tonight, that's for certain.' Fi sighed.

I gasped – the meeting was only a day away. I'd miss my chance to tell everyone about Perijee!

'Isn't there some way we can get there faster?' I asked.

'Yes,' said Fi. 'You just crashed it. Getting you to a sale is the least of our worries now – we need to find food and somewhere to sleep before it gets dark. Somewhere to hide the cow, too.'

'I still don't understand why you stole a cow,' I said.

'Hey!' said Fi, ignoring me. 'Talk about luck – there's a farm, right over there!'

She pointed to the field beside the road. There

was a house in the middle, with smoke coming out of the chimney and clothes flapping on a washing line outside.

'*Jackpot!*' said Fi, patting me on the back. 'Keep an eye out.'

She dashed across the field and started ripping the clothes off the washing line. I ran after her as fast as I could.

'Fi, stop!' I shouted. 'What are you doing?'

'Relax, I'm only taking what I need,' said Fi, pulling on jumper after jumper. 'Come on, let's see what food they've got.'

She ran over to a vegetable patch and started digging up carrots. I grabbed her hands.

'No, Fi!' I said. 'You can't take things that aren't yours!'

Fi raised an eyebrow. 'Why not?'

'Because it's *wrong*,' I said. 'Mum always said . . .'

I trailed off. Just thinking about Mum made me feel weird. She'd always been so good at explaining things I didn't understand – like how you can't ask people why they're bald, or why you have to pay for jam before you eat it. I wondered what she'd think of me now, out here in the middle of nowhere with a thief. I wondered if she'd woken up yet.

'Caitlin,' said Fi. 'That's a nice idea, but that's not how the world works. Not since the Monster turned up, anyway. We *have* to steal things. I mean, look at us: we're in the middle of nowhere, with no food, no place to sleep . . . What else do you suggest we do?'

'Ask the farmer if he'll help us,' I said.

Fi thought about it.

'You know,' she said, 'that's actually a really good idea.'

I smiled. 'Thanks! Well, I'm glad I . . .'

'You could distract the farmer,' said Fi, 'while I sneak into the kitchen and empty his fridge!'

My face fell. 'No, Fi, that's not what I . . .'

'It'll be easy!' She grabbed a piece of paper and pen from her pocket. 'Look – I'll even give you a script. Just say everything I've written down on this piece of paper, and it'll go perfectly.'

I looked down at the paper in horror. The words slipped and shifted in front of me.

'Er . . . no, Fi, I can't . . .'

'Sure you can!' said Fi, ringing the doorbell and leaping behind a bush. 'Just don't screw it up.'

We looked down at the farmer's unconscious body.

'Thanks for knocking him out,' I said.

'It's fine,' said Fi, putting down the shovel.

'Why was he trying to shoot me?' I asked.

'He thought you were a member of Obsidian Blade,' said Fi, picking up the smoking shotgun and dropping it down a drain.

I frowned. 'Obsidi-what?'

'*Obsidian Blade*,' said Fi. 'They're the cult that's running around the countryside, kidnapping people and leaving those weird messages. He thought you were one of them. I think it was when you started saying all those made-up words.'

I blushed furiously. Fi sighed.

'So – you can't read properly, can you?'

I coughed. 'What makes you think I can't read?'

'You were reading the script upside down.'

I stared at the ground.

'Look,' I said. 'I *can* read. Just not quickly. Or well. Especially when I'm nervous.'

Fi shrugged. 'You should have told me. I can teach you.'

I glanced up. 'You can?'

Fi shrugged. 'Sure. I taught myself when I was four, so teaching you will be easy. We'll start tonight.'

I beamed. 'Thanks, Fi. You're a good friend.'

'We're not friends,' said Fi. 'I told you that already.'

'Oh yeah!' I said. 'But we're warming to each other ... right?'

I felt really bad for scaring the farmer, so I made him a sandwich and left it by his head. Then we piled some hot dogs into a handbag, slung them over the cow's back and set off across the fields.

'He's going to come after us,' Fi explained. 'So we'll have to move fast and stay off the main roads. It's not hard to spot, two girls with a cow.'

I sighed. 'I *still* don't get why you stole the ...'

'Hey! *Bingo!*' said Fi, pointing through the trees. 'Look over there – a river! It's *bound* to be the same one that runs through Wanderly!'

We pushed our way through the trees and stood by the river. It was enormous and loud and full of tumbling white water. There were cars and garden sheds floating down the middle of it.

'Wow,' I said. 'That's *massive.*'

'Yep,' said Fi. 'Ever since the Monster blocked it up at the city, it's been bursting its banks and flooding all over the country. Loads of villages are under water now. If you want to get to Wanderly quickly, we'll need a boat.' She pointed up the river. 'That one'll do.'

A luxury yacht was weaving towards us, long and sleek as a limousine. A skull and crossbones had been spraypainted on the front, and the sides were covered in barbed wire. There were six men standing in the back holding rifles.

'Er . . . really?' I said. 'Those men look dangerous, Fi.'

'I know they do,' said Fi. 'That's why we need to get them *off* the boat before we steal it.' She tapped her feet. 'Let's see . . . can't do the "naïve idiot" routine, not on these guys . . . no point trying the old "switch 'n' shove" . . . Any ideas?'

'I've got some superglue,' I said.

Fi rolled her eyes and turned away. I gritted my teeth – this was my chance to prove to her that I wasn't stupid. I watched the yacht get closer and closer. If I didn't think up an idea fast, that was it – I'd *never* get to the meeting in time, and then . . .

I gasped.

'Fi, I've got it! I know how we can steal the boat!'

Fi didn't even turn around. But there was no time to lose – I charged into the woods beside us and got to work. Fi sighed.

'Well, it's no good – I've got nothing. We'll just have to wait until the next boat comes past ... whenever that might be. But if that farmer finds us ...'

She turned round to me and jumped. I was holding a branch above my head. It was three times bigger than me, and also on fire.

'Caitlin!' said Fi. 'What are you *doing*?'

'Relax,' I said. 'I think I've got an idea.'

Eight and a half minutes later Fi and I were speeding down the river in the yacht, with the cow trailing behind in a small rubber dinghy. The men were trying to chase us along the bank, but they weren't doing very well because I'd superglued their feet together.

'Caitlin, that was ... *amazing*!' said Fi. 'How did you come up with that idea?!'

I shrugged. 'I don't know. It just sort of made sense.'

Fi shook her head. 'But I've never seen anything like it! I mean, that bit with the oysters ...'

'I know!'

'... And that song you did ...'

'I didn't even plan that!'

'It was . . . *incredible*,' said Fi, smiling at me. 'Just incredible. You're smarter than I thought, Caitlin.'

I blushed with pride. It was the first time Fi had said anything nice to me – in fact, it was the first time I'd seen her smile. She suddenly realised what she was doing and snapped back to normal.

'Well, enough of that,' she muttered. 'Let's stay focused. Know anything about boats?'

I shrugged. 'A little.'

'Good,' said Fi, handing me the wheel. 'I'm exhausted. Go slow and give me a shout when you spot a big castle by the river – it means we're five miles from Wanderly. It's being used as an army base now, so we'll have to find a way of sneaking past before they shoot us. Night.'

She lay on the floor and pulled an eyemask out of her pocket, snapping it on. I glanced at her. There was something about Fi that was nagging at me – something I'd been wanting to ask her all day.

'Fi?'

'Yes, Caitlin?'

'Have you *always* done this? Walk around the countryside and steal things off people?'

Fi shrugged. 'Pretty much. I've been on the road my whole life.'

'So when you said you taught yourself to read – does that mean you never went to school either?'

Fi snorted. 'Of course I didn't!'

'Didn't your parents mind?'

Fi was silent.

'No, Caitlin,' she said. 'They didn't mind at all.'

I frowned. 'But ... *how*? I mean, if *my* parents found out I wasn't going to school, they'd kill me! Didn't they say anything, or try to stop you, or ...'

'Just watch the river,' Fi snapped, cutting me off. 'The last thing we need is for you to crash into another bridge and get us spotted by the army. Especially when we've got a cow with us.'

I glanced back at the cow. It was wearing a lifejacket and was clearly enjoying itself. I shook my head.

'I *just* don't understand why you stole ...'

'Caitlin,' said Fi calmly, 'if you say that one more time, I am going to kill you.'

'Well,' said Fi, 'I guess *that* makes things a bit easier.'

The castle was completely destroyed. All that was left of the army base was a pile of smoking rubble and a single tower that was barely standing. Across it, in blood-red paint, someone had drawn:

'Obsidian Blade.' Fi sighed. 'Honestly, those guys get *everywhere*.'

'Why did they blow up the castle?' I said.

'Because they're nutters,' said Fi. 'They think the Monster is some kind of god.' She glanced at me.

'They don't just kidnap people, you know – they sacrifice them. Break into their homes in the middle of the night and snatch them out of their beds.'

I shivered. For a moment I was really glad I wasn't on my own. I got the feeling Fi was too – I was sure I saw her step a little bit closer to me.

'Well, we're almost at Wanderly now,' she said. 'Let's dump the boat and camp here tonight. We can walk into town first thing tomorrow.'

Perfect – we were right on time for the meeting, *and* I was going camping! I used to ask Dad if he'd take me all the time, but he never could – he was always too busy. I guessed there'd be plenty of time for stuff like that after I found him again.

I wondered where Dad was now. Maybe he was camping out too somewhere, trying to find me. I wondered what he'd say when he saw me again.

'Well, don't just *stand* there,' said Fi. 'I'm supposed to be teaching you to read – remember?'

I beamed. 'Oh yeah! Shall I light us a campfire?'

'I'm on it,' said Fi, heaving a can of petrol out the cupboard.

I made us two little beds while Fi burned the boat down. It was just like a real campfire but with lots more smoke. We took turns reading the boat safety manual while it sank into the river beside us. I needed lots of help, but Fi was really good at teaching – she didn't ever make me feel stupid, not once.

Afterwards we settled down to a dinner of hot dogs and freshly squeezed milk and watched the river run by. The setting sun wrapped round us like a blanket.

'This is nice,' I said.

'You bet,' said Fi. 'Roaring petrol fire, the open water – *solitude*. Everything you need.'

I looked at her. '. . . Solitude?'

'It means being on your own,' said Fi.

I shifted. I'd never thought anyone would *want* to be on their own.

'Doesn't that mean you get lonely?' I said.

Fi snorted. 'Who cares about being lonely? When you're alone, you're *safe*. It means never having to worry about anyone tricking you or taking your things.'

I frowned. 'Speaking of which, have you seen my hat or—'

'Plus,' Fi interrupted, 'when you're alone, no one can *hurt* you. No one can lie to you or tell you you're worthless. No one can make you do anything you don't want. No one can come home in the middle of the night and start screaming at you.'

Fi trailed off. There was a weird pause.

'Has that actually happened to you?' I said, amazed.

Fi shuffled irritably on the ground.

'Yeah, well,' she muttered. 'What would you know about being lonely?'

Fi kicked at some leaves and we fell silent. It was getting dark now. The Monster had taken down most of the electricity pylons days ago, which meant the night sky was clearer than ever. Above us the stars were beginning to blink into place. Just like when . . .

I smiled. Thinking about Perijee always made me happier.

'I used to be lonely all the time,' I said. 'I don't have any brothers or sisters. Mum and Dad were always too busy to talk to me. Until Perijee came along, I'd never even had a real friend.'

Fi frowned.

'Perijee? Who's Perijee?'

I froze – I'd blown my cover. I had to smooth this over, fast.

'Er . . .'

'Wait – is *that* the reason you're going to Wanderly?' said Fi. 'This "Perijee"?'

'Er . . .'

'I knew there was another reason!' Fi sat up. 'What is he – a boy? A friend? A *boyfriend*?'

'Er . . .'

'Is he anything to do with that photo you keep hidden in your pocket?'

I gasped and reached for the photo. It was already gone. Fi was holding it.

'Hey!' I said. 'How did you . . .'

'My god,' said Fi. 'Caitlin . . . what *is* that?'

I sighed. I couldn't hide the truth from Fi any more. She'd already done so much for me – taken me with her, helped me read . . . she'd even saved my life once or twice. She deserved to know what I was really doing. Besides, I was completely rubbish at lying.

I told her everything. I told her about the day I first found Perijee, and the day the army appeared, and how he changed. By the time I was finished, Fi's eyes were bugging out her head.

'Holy crap,' she said. 'You *knew* the Monster?!'

I shook my head. 'Not really – the Monster is like this . . . horrible thing that grew out of Perijee. Only now Perijee's stuck on top of him and can't get free. *That's* why I'm going to Wanderly – to show everyone that he's actually good, and stop them from trying to kill the Monster.'

127

Fi raised an eyebrow. 'You want to stop them attacking a giant alien that's destroying the world.'

'Exactly,' I said. 'Then I'm going to find Dad, wherever he is, and together we'll go to the city and save Perijee. And then we'll find a way of getting him back into space.' I beamed. 'You can come too, if you like.'

Fi stared at me. Then she fell over laughing.

'Caitlin,' she snorted, '*come on!* That's impossible! I mean, even if you *do* manage to get anyone on your side, you'll never be able to find your dad, let alone travel to the most dangerous place in the world . . . !'

I looked at her, confused.

'But I have to, Fi. I *promised* Perijee I'd get him home, no matter what it took. That's what friends do, right? So even if it's hard or dangerous . . . well, I have to try.'

Fi was stunned. Neither of us spoke for ages. Eventually the cow broke the tension by farting.

'Right,' said Fi, rubbing her head. She had gone a bit pale. 'I'm, er . . . going to bed. I've got a lot to think about. You?'

I shook my head. 'Thanks, but I'm going to look at the stars for a bit. You could never see them in camp. You know – because of the ceiling.'

'You do that,' said Fi, and turned away without another word.

I smiled. Fi might not always be the easiest person to live with, or the politest, and she *was* stealing my stuff off me, but I was still really glad she was there.

I lay on my back and gazed at the stars. They were beautiful – they looked exactly the same as they did back on Middle Island, when Perijee and me used to watch them together on the beach. Which is weird, when you think about it – that the stars would be the same, even though we'd gone so far and so much had changed.

I remembered when we used to walk hand in hand along the water's edge, and Perijee would make himself glow like a lantern so that I could see where I was going. I hugged myself tight. I'd have given anything to see him again, right then.

I wondered if Perijee was thinking about me too. I hoped he was. I wondered if he'd worked out what the symbols on his body meant yet.

I rolled over to get some sleep, and stopped. There on the ground beside me were my hat and watch, all folded up in a little pile. The photo of me and Perijee was on top. I turned to Fi.

'Thanks, Fi,' I said. 'You're a good friend.'

Fi didn't say anything. She was fast asleep.

Wanderly was packed. Everyone from miles and miles around was squeezing down the main road, their arms full of suitcases and shotguns and standard lamps. I was amazed. I'd never seen so many people in one place before.

'Terrible, isn't it?' said Fi. 'The army have given up trying to help anyone – even those who've lost their homes. Most people here have nowhere left to go. They're confused, lost, desperate . . .' She sighed. 'Oh yes. I am going to make an absolute *fortune*.'

I smiled. I was really going to miss Fi.

'Well, good luck with your cow,' I said, shaking her hand. 'It was really nice getting to know you. Hopefully we can hang out again sometime when the world is not ending.'

Fi's face fell. 'What? Where are you going?'

'The meeting's about to start,' I said. 'I've got to

tell everyone about Perijee. Besides – you said we'd split up when we got here.'

Fi shoved my hand away. 'Forget that! There's no *way* you're going to that meeting on your own, Caitlin, they'll eat you alive.' She put her arm around me. 'If you're going, I'm going. That's what friends do – right?'

I almost glowed.

'Did you just say we're friends?'

'Yeah, yeah,' said Fi, rolling her eyes. 'We're friends.'

'... *Best* friends?'

'Don't push your luck.'

Finding the meeting was easy – everyone was cramming into a massive building in the centre of town. Fi locked the cow in a bike rack and we pushed our way inside.

It was an enormous theatre. Everyone was fighting for the last few spaces, sitting on the backs of chairs and pulling each other up onto ledges. The balconies and boxes were already heaving. I jumped up and down but it was no use – I couldn't see a thing. How was I going to tell everyone about Perijee if they couldn't even see me?

'I'll get you a seat,' said Fi.

She pulled a plastic bag out of her pocket and started fake vomiting into it. Within seconds everyone in the nearest row had left. I was impressed.

'Wow,' I said. 'That was disgusting.'

'You're welcome,' said Fi. 'Now, if you don't mind, I have some work to do before your speech. It's a pickpocket's paradise in here – I reckon I'll make a wallet a minute, maybe two if they're drunk. Good luck!'

She disappeared into the crowd and I sat down excitedly, clutching the photograph to my chest. There was no *way* anyone could see this picture and not believe Perijee was worth saving – he looked so sweet and harmless. I couldn't believe how much I missed him already.

'*Order!*'

A man was stood at the front of the stage. He was burly and unshaven, and looked like he hadn't slept in days.

'Order!' he bellowed, waving his hands over the crowd. 'Order ... ord— Come on everyone, please! We'll never get anything sorted unless we – *all – stop – talking!*'

Everyone fell quiet. The speaker sighed with relief.

'That's better. Now, let's start things off by . . .'

'Kill the Monster!' someone shouted.

The crowd behind me cheered. I turned round – at the back of the theatre I could see dozens of people from the camp, all waving signs with pictures of the Monster being blown up. The speaker waved them all quiet.

'Oi!' he said. 'No shouting out! I *know* we're all frightened, but we're here to save the world! That means we need to spend time discussing the pros and cons of each and every choice before . . .'

'There's no time for that!' screamed someone at the front, holding up a pitchfork. 'We're all going to die! Kill the Monster!'

The rest of the row beside him stood up and cheered, waving more pitchforks. I gulped – it looked like people were really frightened about the Monster. I clearly had my work cut out for me. The speaker waved his hands again.

'Hey! What did I say earlier?' he snapped. 'No pitchforks! We can't have *another* meeting descend into – hey! What are you doing? *Stop that . . . !*'

An hour later we all filed back into the theatre. The speaker glared angrily at us from the stage. He'd been bandaged up pretty well and luckily still had most of his hair.

'Right,' he said. 'I think we can all agree that got out of hand.'

Everyone nodded, embarrassed.

'So from now on,' he said, holding up a pitchfork from the big pile he'd confiscated, 'no one talks unless they're holding the Discussion Pitchfork. Agreed?'

Everyone nodded.

'Good,' he said. 'Now, before we start discussing what we're going to do, let me explain the current situation with the Monster.'

A map of the country unfurled across the back of the stage. Someone had drawn a picture of the Monster over the city, his body winding to the coast like a snake. I was shocked – I had no idea how big he was now. For a moment, I felt just as scared as everyone else.

'As we all know, the Monster's growing bigger every day,' said the speaker. 'His tail now stretches from the city all the way to the sea. The army have built a blockade of ships around his head, but so far they've done nothing to stop him.'

Everyone grumbled angrily. Another map dropped over the first one. It showed the Monster's body squiggling across the world's oceans like a bowl of noodles.

'The Monster's tail has also split into thousands of smaller tentacles,' said the speaker. 'They run along the ocean floor, and are slowly spreading across the entire world. More and more are growing each day. They appear to be ... looking for something.'

I was shocked – I must have missed all this while I was on the road with Fi. I'd seen the tentacles on the news, of course, but I had no idea they were *looking* for something. What on earth were they looking for?

'And that's not the only change,' said the speaker. 'I'm sure we've all seen the recent pictures of the small white creature they spotted on top of the Monster's head a few days ago ...'

I gasped – they knew about Perijee! I clutched the photo even tighter to my chest. This was it – they *had* to listen to me now. The moment I got the Discussion Pitchfork, I'd tell them everything.

'No one knows *what* the white creature is,' the speaker explained. 'But ever since it appeared ...' His face darkened. 'Well, it's changed the situation for the worse.'

Another map of the country unfurled across the back of the stage. This one had dozens of little red Xs all over it, getting closer and closer to the city. People started muttering nervously around me.

'These Xs,' said the speaker, pointing to the map, 'are all sightings of different cults from the last few days. All the best-known ones have been spotted: the End of the World Appreciation Club, Apocalypse Anonymous ... And as you can see, they're all heading straight for the city. They've been sneaking through the army blockade to get closer to the Monster – this morning, news cameras even spotted them climbing onto his back.'

The crowd didn't like this at all – and neither did I. Why were people heading towards Perijee? What if they were trying to hurt him?

'But that's not the worst part,' said the speaker, clearing his throat. 'We've all noticed the recent increase in messages left by ... *Obsidian Blade*.' He swallowed. 'It seems – well, it seems they're heading towards the city as well.'

This caused an absolute fit in the crowd. Everyone started shouting over each other, demanding to speak. A man in the front row stood up and grabbed the Discussion Pitchfork.

'Then what are we waiting for?' he cried. 'Those psychos have to be stopped – they could be trying to help the Monster take over the world right now!' He turned to the room, Pitchfork held high. 'I say we do what the army should have done from the start, and blow them all to smithereens! The Monster, the white creature, Obsidian Blade . . . *Death to them all!*'

This got the biggest cheer yet. It was no good waiting for my turn with the Pitchfork – I had to tell them the truth right away. I jumped up onto my seat, waving the photo above my head.

'Wait – everyone listen!' I shouted. 'You're all wrong – the white creature isn't bad, he's good! He just wants to go home! Everyone look at this photo, *please*!'

I shouted and shouted . . . but no one even noticed me. They were all too busy arguing with each other about the best way to kill the Monster – by planting a bomb in his brain, or by setting him on fire, or by cutting him into a thousand pieces. The speaker wrestled back the Discussion Pitchfork.

'Enough discussion!' he shouted. 'Time to vote. All those in favour of destroying the Monster?'

The roar from the crowd was enormous. I looked at them in shock – almost every single hand was up in the air. Frank had been right all along. The world *did* want Perijee dead. I sank back into the chair, my eyes filling with tears.

'Oh Perijee,' I whispered. 'I'm so sorry. I tried.'

'Then that settles it!' said the speaker, waving his hands over the jeering crowd. 'We'll start planning our attack right away!' He smiled sarcastically. 'Unless, of course ... there's anyone opposed?'

'*I am!*'

The shout cut through the room like a gunshot.

'*I* oppose the killing!'

I spun round. An old lady was standing on her seat in the middle of the theatre. She was wearing a cardigan with pearl buttons and a pair of glasses that sat on the end of her nose. She looked lovely – not like the sort of person who stood on her seat and shouted.

'And *all* of you should do the same!'

The audience was speechless – and so was I. The only sound in the room was someone complaining that their wallet had just been stolen. The speaker shuffled awkwardly on the stage.

'Er ... sorry, you'll need to wait for your turn with the Discussion Pitchfork ...'

'Listen to us!' said the old lady, ignoring him. 'Have we forgotten how to be human? This is no "monster" we're talking about – this is a *living creature*! We should be finding out why he's here, *talking* to him – not *destroying* him!'

I couldn't believe it. Someone wanted to help Perijee. Someone *cared*. The old lady pulled herself up to her full height.

'I belong to a group,' she announced, 'who believe in living side by side with our visitor. Together we will travel to the city and welcome him to this planet – not with guns, or with bombs, but with *love*!'

She held out her arms.

'Come, all of you, before it's too late – our boat leaves first thing tomorrow! *JOIN US!*'

There was a moment of stunned silence – and then the whole room burst into hysterics, pointing and laughing at the old lady. Someone jumped out of their seat beside me.

'Listen to her!' he cried. 'Poor creature . . . *Love?* She's a nutter!'

The old lady looked around in shock – then her face hardened. She leapt from her chair and barged her way to the exit. No one in the audience seemed to notice her leaving – they were too busy roaring with laughter.

Except me. I was staring at the exit where she had just left, my heart pounding.

'She's going to the city,' I gasped. 'She ... she wants to help Perijee!'

Fi suddenly appeared beside me, her hands piled high with wallets.

'*Phew!* Thirty-six!' she said. 'That has *got* to be a record.'

I jumped up and grabbed her hand, dragging her to the doors.

'Hey!' said Fi. 'Where are you going?'

'To the river!' I shouted. 'We've got a boat to catch!'

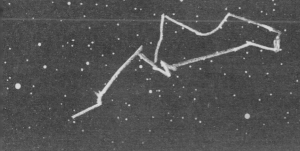

I t was the biggest boat I'd ever seen.

It had taken us all day to find it. It was a paddle steamer, three storeys high, looming out the water like an iceberg. It didn't look like the sort of boat an old lady would use, but I knew it was hers because the windows were covered in flower baskets and stickers about cat charities.

'Caitlin,' said Fi, 'are you out of your mind?'

She was standing on the bank beside me, looking unimpressed.

'You can't just go to the most dangerous place in the world in ... *that*!'

I sighed. 'She's the only one who doesn't want Perijee dead. I have to go with her.'

Fi was stunned. 'So ... that's it? You're going to leave me behind for a load of strangers?'

'Of course not!' I said. 'You're coming with me.'

I ran up the gangplank and knocked on the door before Fi could argue.

'It'll be fun!' I said. 'It's not every day you get to save the world. And anyway, she's not a *stranger* – she's an old lady! Old ladies are nice.'

The door swung open and a head poked out. It was the old lady from the meeting. She looked me up and down.

'Yes?' she said sharply. 'What do you want?'

I gave her my most winning smile. 'I heard what you said about the Monster – I want to join your group!'

She rolled her eyes.

'Absolutely not,' she said. 'You can't be more than ten years old. Go away.'

My face fell. She wasn't anything like she'd been in the meeting – she was rude and mean. She even tried to slam the door in my face, but I wasn't going to let her get away so easily. I jammed my foot inside and pulled the photo out my pocket.

'But look – I know more about the Monster than anyone!' I thrust the photo at her. 'That's me, standing right next to the white creature! He's my friend – my brother!'

The old lady squinted at the photo. Then she fell

straight out the door like all the strings holding her up had been cut. I grinned.

'So . . . can we come with you?'

The old lady was lost for words. She was almost shaking.

'W-wait here!' she gabbled.

She ran inside and slammed the door behind her, leaving me and Fi stood awkwardly on the gangplank.

'You're right,' said Fi. 'She seems lovely.'

I shrugged. 'Well . . . I dunno. Maybe she's a bit demented.'

'Who, her in the massive paddleboat?' said Fi. 'Never.'

The door swung open again and the old lady stepped back outside. This time she looked totally different. She was smiling.

'Goodness!' she said sweetly. 'Where *are* my manners? Of *course* you can come, dearie! Right this way – please!'

She held open the door and bowed down to me, the smile chiselled onto her face like a crack in a plate. I didn't need telling twice – I ran straight inside. She tried to shut the door behind me, but Fi scrambled before she could.

'Not so fast!' she said. 'If Caitlin's going, I'm going too!'

'We're best friends,' I explained.

'No we're not,' she muttered.

I don't know what Fi was so worried about. The inside of the boat was just like any other old lady's house. Everywhere you turned were doilies and porcelain hedgehogs and watercolour paintings of kittens. I felt safer already.

'My name is Margaret,' said the old lady, shaking my hand. 'Sorry for the, er, misunderstanding, my dear – we weren't expecting anyone to join us after our offer was so *rudely* rejected. Come – let me introduce you to the others!'

She hurried me down a corridor lined with bedrooms. I couldn't believe my eyes – in every doorway stood an old woman, wearing a lacy nightgown and with her hair in rollers. There were dozens of them. They all peered out excitedly, whispering to each other and pinching my cheek.

'Wow!' I said. 'I've never seen so many old ladies!'

Margaret smiled. 'There are plenty more amazing things on board, dearie. Here – look at this.'

She came to a door at the end of a corridor – but it

was no ordinary door. It was carved with thousands of letters that spiralled in a great ring across the wood. It looked like a spider's web.

'Do you see what that says?' Margaret asked.

She pointed to the word carved right in the centre. The letters spun in front of me. I flushed with embarrassment.

'Er . . . it says . . . it says . . .'

Fi quickly stepped forwards and took my hand.

'"LOVE",' she said. 'It says "LOVE" – doesn't it, Caitlin?'

I sighed with relief. I was so glad Fi was there.

'Oh, yeah!' I said. 'Of course – LOVE. Why's it written on the door?'

Margaret smiled. 'Love is very important to us, girls – especially to our leader. You will see her in a moment. She is one of the most special people you are ever likely to meet. You should consider yourselves very lucky . . . Most people don't even know she exists!'

She threw open the door and pushed me inside.

'Mother!' she cried. 'This is the girl!'

I fell sprawling into the room, so fast I lost my balance. But just before I hit the floor, a hand shot out and grabbed me. The grip was strong, and safe, and warm.

'A nasty fall you nearly had there,' said a voice.

I looked up. Sat in an armchair in front of me was the biggest woman I had ever seen in my life. She was massive, like a house or a hill is massive. The arms beneath the lace of her nightgown were thick as pillars.

'Are you hurt?' she said gently.

I was speechless. I'd never seen anything so big or so old before. She looked more like a tree than a person. She put me back on my feet and dusted me off.

'No harm done,' she said. 'And what a pleasure to have such life on board for once! My name is Mother – at least, that is what the women call me. You may call me that too, if you wish.'

The word caught me by surprise – *Mum*. By now she'd have worked out I wasn't in camp. She'd probably be beside herself. Suddenly all I could think about was her voice and her hair and the jumper she always wore round the house . . .

I shook my head. I couldn't think about any of that now – I had more important things to do. I had to save Perijee.

'Er . . . thanks,' I said, shaking her hand. 'Nice to meet you, Mother. My name's Caitlin.'

Mother smiled, her face creasing into a thousand wrinkles. 'And your friend?'

I glanced behind me. Fi stood in the doorway, staring at Mother openmouthed.

'Oh yeah!' I said. 'This is . . .'

'Queenie,' said Fi quickly.

I almost said something, but Fi gave me a dark look. I had no idea why she was lying. Luckily Mother didn't seem to notice – she barely gave Fi a nod before turning back to me.

'Margaret tells me you have a very interesting photograph, Caitlin.' She leaned towards me, the chair creaking beneath her. 'May I see it?'

I handed it over nervously. Mother held the photo at arm's length, her eyes sparkling.

'My goodness,' she said quietly. 'What an *exquisite* creature! I've been all around the world, but I've never seen anything quite like him. What a treasure!'

My chest swelled with pride. It felt so good to hear someone say nice things about Perijee for a change. And Mother had so many of them – words just flowed out of her, like hot water from a tap.

'However did you find such an angel?' she asked.

I told her everything. I told her about the meteor shower, and about Perijee arriving on the island, and the day he changed. Mother listened patiently until I was done.

'Extraordinary,' she said. 'You say the Monster just . . . *grew* out of him?'

'Whenever he was frightened,' I said. 'I think that's the problem. He must be terrified, stuck up there by himself. But if someone was nice to him again – if I could talk to him, just for a bit – then the Monster would disappear like it did before, I'm sure of it. And then we can get Perijee home!' I beamed. 'So – will you help us?'

Mother nodded, her eyes lost in thought for a moment. She turned to Fi.

'Queenie, my dear,' she said. 'I'd like to have a private word with Caitlin for a moment. Can you wait outside, please?'

Fi's eyes flicked between me and Mother. For a second, I could have sworn she looked a little jealous.

'Sure,' she said huffily. 'Whatever.'

She walked out the door and Margaret quickly closed it behind her. Mother smiled at me.

'I thought it would be best if we talked alone, Caitlin,' she said. 'Seeing as no one knows Perijee better than you. You've been a wonderful friend to him.'

I shrugged. 'Well, I guess I ...'

'Do you love him?'

She asked me so quickly that for a second I didn't know what to say. She reached out and held my face.

'*Love*,' she said. 'I can see it in you, my dear, bright as the sun. You've already come so far – why do it, if not for love?'

The room was changing around me. It was as if everything was hovering a centimetre off the floor, and Mother was holding me in place with just her eyes.

'Love is the most important thing there is, Caitlin,' she said, almost in a whisper. 'But there's not much of it left – not real love, not nowadays. A girl who loves like you do is precious. A girl like you can save the world.'

I'd never been called special before – not by anyone. My heart swelled. Mother's words kept washing over me like waves on a warm ocean.

'But love is not always enough, Caitlin,' she said. 'If you truly want to save your friend, you must be prepared to leave everything behind. Your home, your family ...' Her eyes stayed locked on mine. 'Even your friend Queenie, if it comes to it.'

I snapped awake – what did she mean? I couldn't

leave Fi behind, not after everything she had done for me. She was my *friend* . . .

'It is the only way, Caitlin,' said Mother, leaning closer. 'You must forget *everything* except him. You do love him – don't you?'

Mother was right. If I didn't get to Perijee in time, he could die. And Fi . . . well, Fi was different, wasn't she? She could look after herself. She didn't need me like Perijee did.

'Can you do it, Caitlin?' said Mother, her face only inches from mine. 'Can you give up everything to save him?'

I nodded. 'Yes. I can.'

Mother leapt out her chair and the room slammed back to normal. It was like falling out of bed in the middle of a dream. I could finally see how huge she was – how she filled the room with just her shadow. She didn't even look that old any more.

'Margaret!' she boomed. 'Find Caitlin the best room we have! Forget waiting for more followers – we leave for the city immediately!'

The old ladies cheered as Margaret led Fi and me to our new bedroom, fighting each other to shake my hand. Inside were two cosy beds with silk sheets, piled high with cushions. It looked like something from a fancy hotel. I waited until everyone had left before leaping onto the nearest bed.

'Can you believe it, Fi?' I laughed, jumping up and down. 'We've done it – a first-class ticket straight to Perijee! Give me an *F*! Give me an *E*! Give me a . . .'

'You shouldn't have said yes,' said Fi angrily. 'Not while I was out the room. You could have agreed to *anything*.'

I stopped jumping.

'. . . What do you mean?'

Fi pulled me off the bed.

'Look, I don't trust these women. Something's not right, I can feel it. Let's go – we can get to the city ourselves. Just you and me.'

She was holding me a bit harder than I liked. I pulled away. She was acting just like Mum – treating me like I couldn't think for myself.

'But Fi, I *want* to go,' I said. 'They're really nice. They want to help Perijee, and they can get there quicker than anyone else. I mean, if you don't want to come with us . . .'

Fi looked like she'd been slapped.

'"Us" now, is it?' she said. 'So after everything we've done together – after all that stuff you said about being my friend – you'd just go without me?'

I'd never heard Fi sound so upset before. Suddenly I felt terrible.

'Fi, I didn't . . .'

'No, it's fine,' she said coldly. 'At least I know where I stand. Well, I'd better go get the cow before you and your new friends leave me behind.'

She marched out without another word. I watched her go, my head spinning. We'd been getting on great a few minutes before – and now she was angry with me. I had no idea friends were so complicated!

But there was no point being upset now – I was going to see Perijee again. My heart soared just thinking about it. Soon we'd be back together. Sure, Fi was mad at me, but she couldn't be mad forever . . . and soon I'd be able to find Dad and save the world. Everything had turned out perfect.

There was just *one* thing that didn't make sense.

When one of the old ladies had reached out to shake my hand, the sleeve of her nightgown had slipped up. She'd quickly pulled it down again – but a second too late. I had already seen her arm underneath.

It was completely covered in tattoos.

I woke bright and early, the sun streaming through the window and the riverbank rolling past in clouds of boat steam. I sat up and looked around. Fi was nowhere to be seen.

Eventually I found her outside on the deck, fast asleep on top of the cow. I shook her awake.

'Fi, I'm really sorry about last night,' I said. 'I made you this.'

It was an old bobble hat I'd found in a cupboard. It was just like mine, except I'd written F̶I̶ QEENY on the front in marker pen.

'I didn't know how to spell "Best Friend",' I said. 'We ... we are still friends, aren't we?'

'Gerroff, s'my cow,' Fi muttered, and fell back asleep.

I smiled. I knew that meant yes.

I got bored trying to wake her up, so I searched

153

the boat until I found the door to Mother's room. In the daylight I could see the carvings in the wood properly. There was *LOVE*, written in the centre just like before . . . but the letters around it were different. They weren't letters – they were symbols. Kind of like the ones on Perijee's body.

'Weird,' I said.

I pushed open the door and stepped inside. All the old ladies were standing round a big table covered in papers.

'Morning everyone!' I said. 'What are you all doing?'

The women swung round and glared at me. I was surprised – they'd been so happy to see me the night before, but now they looked pretty hacked off. The only one who wasn't angry was Mother.

'Come in, my girl!' she boomed. 'Come right inside – there are no secrets from our guests here!'

She pulled me over to the table and swept her arm across the papers.

'Behold – our plans to save the world!'

My face fell. Every single sheet was covered with numbers and letters that swirled and twisted in front of me.

'Well?' said Mother. 'What do you think, child?'

I blushed furiously.

'I . . . I don't know what they say,' I said.

Mother shrugged. 'Well, why don't you read me the bit you don't understand, and I'll explain it to you?'

My face burned.

'I – I can't,' I said. 'I'm no good at reading.'

There was an awful pause. For a moment I thought that Mother was going to laugh at me. But she didn't.

'Come on, then!' she said. 'Let me show you.'

She picked me up and plonked me on her lap. I was shocked – no one had done that to me in years. I thought I'd be a bit embarrassed, but I wasn't. It felt really good. Mother leaned over the table.

'This is a map showing our way to the city.' She pointed to a sheet in front of her. 'Can you see?'

She ran her finger along a blue line, and suddenly it all made sense. I nodded.

'We'll arrive at the Monster's head in two days,' Mother explained, tracing the line across the map. 'And not a moment too soon. We have just received information that the army is finally organising an attack – a missile air strike, aimed directly at his brain.'

I gasped. 'But . . . that's right where Perijee is!'

'Indeed, my girl,' said Mother sadly. 'That's why

it's full steam ahead, night and day, until we reach the blockade.'

Her finger came to a stop at the ring of warships surrounding the Monster's head. I frowned.

'. . . And then what?' I said. 'How are we going to get past the boats?'

At that moment the door opened and Fi walked in. I knew right away we were friends again – she was wearing my hat!

'F— I mean, Queenie!' I said, waving at her. 'Come look at our plans . . . !'

But before Fi could take another step, the old ladies tore the papers from the table and started stuffing them into boxes. This time Mother didn't try to stop them.

'Ah, yes,' she said, her voice cold. '*Queenie*, was it? I almost forgot about you. So nice of you to finally join us.'

Fi smiled back, hard as granite. 'Yeah, sorry for butting in – just thought I'd keep an eye on things. Seeing as I'm Caitlin's friend and everything.'

The two of them stared at each other in grim silence. It was like they were talking to each other in some secret language I didn't understand. It was really awkward – they obviously didn't like each other.

'Er ... should I get down now?' I said.

Mother nodded. 'Yes, child. The two of you should leave us ladies alone to the planning.'

She plonked me back on my feet.

'But make sure you're in the dining room for six o'clock. We're holding a special dinner in your honour, Caitlin! To celebrate your arrival, and the beginning of our mission to save Perijee.' She gave Fi a steely glance. 'I'm sure we can find an extra chair for Queenie.'

The ladies gave me a round of applause while Fi fumed. I felt really bad for her – Mother was giving me loads of attention and I could tell it was upsetting Fi. The last thing I wanted was for us to have another argument.

'Great idea!' I said, taking Fi's hand. 'And F— I mean, *Queenie* can sit right next to me. Can't she, Mother?'

Mother nodded. 'You're the guest of honour, child – you can have anything you want.'

I froze.

'Can I choose what we eat, too?'

'Of course!' said Mother. 'Choose whatever you fancy – anything in the whole wide world!'

*

I slammed the pan onto the table.

'It's called Caitlin's Perfect Pasta.'

It'd been so long since I'd last cooked, I'd forgotten how much I loved it. The boat's kitchen didn't have all the things I needed, but like all the best chefs I made do. There was no tomato ketchup so I used brown sauce, and instead of herbs I just pulled up some grass from the riverbank.

'Wow,' said Fi. 'I've never seen food look like that before.'

'Thanks!' I said.

The dinner was great – Mother and Fi were sat too far apart to argue, and everyone loved the food. You could tell because no one talked! They say that's the sign people are enjoying their meal. The only sound was the scraping of chairs every few seconds while someone ran to the toilet.

'What a feast!' said Mother, even though she had only eaten one spoonful before saying she was full. 'Such a talented girl. Your mother must be very proud of you, Caitlin!'

I almost dropped my fork.

'Why, if I had a daughter like you, I'd be the proudest mother in the whole ...'

'Thanks,' I said, desperate to change the subject

to something that didn't make me want to be sick. 'Um . . . do you guys have a TV on board?'

It was like I'd flicked a switch. Everyone fell silent. All the old women stopped what they were doing and looked at Mother. I'd obviously said something wrong. I shuffled nervously on my seat.

'Sorry – I thought we could watch the news, that's all. To see if Perijee's on. I haven't seen him in ages.'

The women glanced at each other. It was strange – they were almost always silent, waiting to see what Mother would do or say next. I hardly ever saw them speak. Mother pushed her plate away with a sigh.

'A fine idea, my girl,' she said. 'But I'm afraid it's not possible. There's no TV on board.'

Fi looked up in surprise.

'No TV? *Really?*'

Mother gritted her teeth. '*Yes*, Queenie, that's what I said – no TV.' She glanced at her watch. 'In fact, it's getting late. Maybe the little chef *and her charming friend* should go to bed before . . .'

'What about the one you've got hidden in that cupboard over there?' said Fi, pointing behind her.

One of the old women spat out her food. Mother's eyes widened with shock. Fi grinned.

'I found it while looking round the boat earlier,'

she said. 'Seems odd that you would forget about something like that.'

Mother glared at Fi like she wanted to rip her to pieces. I coughed nervously – the mood in the room was turning bad again. I didn't want it to get any worse.

'So . . . can we watch the news?' I asked. 'Just for a bit?'

Mother gripped her butter knife.

'Of course!' she said. 'I completely forgot about that old thing – you know what old ladies are like, ha ha! Yes, a few minutes of TV is fine – but then straight to bed, please. We'll be at the city in a matter of days, and the women and I need to discuss our plans for the Monster.'

She snapped her fingers. The old ladies obediently leapt up and wheeled out the TV from the cupboard, fiddling with the buttons. Mother was right – it was pretty old. She must have simply forgotten it was there.

But something she'd said didn't seem right.

'. . . Mother?'

She smiled sweetly. 'Yes, child?'

'What *are* your plans for the Monster? I thought . . . I thought we were going to the city to talk to Perijee. What does the Monster have to do with anything?'

The women fell silent again. Fi and Mother locked eyes across the table. The screen slipped in and out of static behind them, shapes flashing up for a moment before disappearing.

'Well, that all depends, my girl,' said Mother carefully. 'What if the Monster doesn't go away after you've saved Perijee?'

The TV hissed and crackled. I hadn't really thought about that.

'Well ... we could find my dad,' I said. 'He'll know what to do.'

Mother nodded. 'Your father – the scientist.'

'Yeah!' I said. 'He's an expert on aliens. The one who's going to help me get Perijee home – remember?'

Things were beginning to emerge on the screen now – people, colours, things moving. Mother shared a look with the women. Then she leaned across the table towards me.

'But, my dear girl,' she said, 'do you even know where your father *is*?'

The screen suddenly flashed clear. I dropped my glass.

'*Dad?!*'

He was right there, looking at me out of the TV.

'And with us tonight,' the newsreader was ... saying, 'we have Dr Paul Bennett, the leading world expert on the Monster.'

I was speechless. Dad was sitting in a chair, wearing a suit, adjusting his glasses. Why was he on TV? Why wasn't he out looking for me?

One of the old ladies went to turn off the TV, but Mother waved her away furiously. On-screen, the newsreader turned to Dad.

'I suppose the first question on everyone's mind, Dr Bennett, is simply: what is the Monster? Where has he come from?'

Dad smoothed his tie. 'The answer is obvious – it comes from an alien species that lays its eggs on meteors. A section of rock containing one of these eggs must have broken off during the recent meteor shower and fallen through our atmosphere, after which the egg hatched on land. There's no other possible explanation for the timing of the Monster's first appearance.'

The newsreader leaned forwards.

'And this is the most incredible part of the story, isn't it, Dr Bennett? The part where you *yourself* discover the Monster, on the beach of your island home!'

The words hit my stomach and stayed there.

'It really was a once-in-a-lifetime moment,' said Dad proudly. 'I was out for my walk – having just dropped my daughter off at school, like I do every morning – and there he was, right in front of me!'

I couldn't believe it – he was lying. Why would he *lie* about something like that?

'Of course,' said Dad, 'I go into all the details in the latest edition of my book, published today.'

He held one up to the camera. On the front cover there was a picture of him stepping on the Monster's head and crushing it to a paste.

'Inside you'll get the full story – how I taught the Monster to speak, how I know it better than anyone …' He smiled to the camera. 'But most importantly of all, how it can be *destroyed*.'

I sat in silence, the pain in my stomach getting sharper and sharper. I guess I shouldn't have been so surprised. It was just like Mum had said – I knew what Dad was like. He'd always put his work before everything else. Of course he would never have searched the country for me – he probably hadn't even noticed I was gone. I couldn't believe I'd been so . . .

'Stupid,' I said quietly.

My eyes were welling up. Fi held my hand.

'Caitlin . . . are you all right?'

I nodded. 'Yeah. I just . . . I can't believe he'd give up on Perijee like that.'

Mother reached across the table and took my other hand.

'Oh, my poor girl,' she said. 'I am so sorry. There is *nothing* worse than being failed by your own family – believe me, I know.' She nodded to the rest of the table. 'But look around you, child! Look who you're with! Who needs family when you have us?'

I looked down the table. Mother was right – I had Fi sat right beside me, and a sea of warm smiling faces in front. It didn't matter if Dad had let me down – I didn't need him any more. Not when I had so many new friends.

Here on this boat, I was the safest I'd been in my whole . . .

'*BREAKING NEWS!*'

The TV slammed back to the newsroom, a

reporter glaring down the camera.

'Another bloody attack by Obsidian Blade!'

The old ladies flew from their chairs to turn off the TV, but they were so panicked they crashed into each other and ripped the dial off the front. Mother threw the entire table to one side and charged forwards, but she was too late. I watched as the camera slowly panned round the smouldering remains of a burned-out building.

It was the theatre in Wanderly.

There was nothing left – only a single blackened wall where the stage had been. The scorched map hung in tatters at the back. Across it, in blood-red paint that pooled into greasy ashes, someone had drawn:

The TV turned black. Mother stood beside it, her face white, the plug hanging from her fist.

Her arms were bare where her nightgown had ripped. They were covered in tattoos from shoulder to wrist – black tentacles twisting into the symbol I'd just seen on TV.

'. . . *You?*' I whispered. '*You're* Obsidian Blade?'

The old ladies stood rooted to the spot. Mother stepped forwards.

'My child—'

I scrambled out my chair.

'No! I know all about you!' I pointed at her with a trembling hand. 'You're the ones who go around blowing up buildings and sneaking into people's houses and . . . *sacrificing them!*'

Mother clapped a hand to her chest.

'*Sacrificing* people? Is *that* what you think we do, child?'

She burst out laughing, a rich warm laugh that bounced off the walls like a bell.

'Good heavens! No wonder you look so frightened!'

The other women started laughing along with her. I looked at them in confusion – I had no idea what was supposed to be so funny. I glanced over at Fi, but she looked as mystified as I did. She was pressed against the wall behind me, her sharp black eyes flicking between Mother and the exit.

'It is true,' said Mother. 'We *are* the group known as Obsidian Blade. I am sorry we had to hide the truth

166

from you . . . But of course, there is no need to hide anything now.' She nodded to the others. 'Ladies?'

One by one they ripped the arms off their nightgowns and showed me the skin underneath. Every single one was covered in tattoos of winding black tentacles.

'We are an ancient organisation that is dedicated to protecting the Monster,' Mother explained. 'At least, that is what most people call him. They say that he is evil and that he must be destroyed – but they are wrong. They do not understand what he truly *is*.'

'What do you mean?' I said.

Mother nodded and the women instantly bowed their heads. When she spoke her voice was soft and quiet, like a prayer.

'Thousands of years ago, a sacred prophecy was written by the first priests of Obsidian Blade,' she said. 'A prediction that one day a powerful creature will appear on Earth. His body will be covered in words that will answer all questions. And when the time is right, he will take us all to a better place – to paradise, my girl.'

I stared at her in amazement. I couldn't believe what I was hearing.

'. . . You think the creature is *Perijee*?' I said.

Mother nodded. 'That is why we must protect him, child. He is more important than anyone realises.'

I looked at the TV. All I could think about was the blood-red message scrawled across the stage wall.

'But . . . you blew up the theatre,' I said. 'And the castle. You could have hurt someone.'

Mother leaned towards me.

'Soldiers are being trained to blow him up in two days' time, Caitlin. How is that any different?'

'But . . . Perijee wouldn't want anyone *hurt*,' I said. 'I taught him killing things is wrong.'

Mother looked surprised.

'You said you would do *anything* for him, Caitlin.'

I shook my head. 'Not that.'

Mother gazed at me, her face calm and expressionless. Then she nodded.

'As you wish,' she said. 'We'll stop the attacks. From now on, no one else will be hurt.' She held out a hand. 'I give you my word, Caitlin . . .'

'Don't touch her!'

Fi leapt forwards, grabbing my arm and pulling me away from Mother.

'She's a maniac, Caitlin! We have to get out of here!'

I frowned. 'But . . . she just said she's not going to hurt anyone else. She *promised* . . .'

'You can't believe a word she says!' said Fi. 'She's lied to you, and she'll lie again!'

Suddenly Mother was on her knees in front of me, gripping my other arm.

'I admit it, child,' she said. 'I lied – and it was a terrible mistake. You must stay with us. Without you, we cannot save Perijee.'

I looked between the two of them in shock. I had no idea what to do.

'Caitlin, *come on!*' cried Fi, pulling me hard. 'We have to go . . .'

'You *must* stay, child . . .'

I closed my eyes. In my mind I could see Perijee on top of the Monster's head – frightened, lost, alone. On the ground below him were thousands of people like the ones in Wanderly, waving pitchforks and screaming for him to be killed. And in the air above him were a hundred planes, swooping down and firing their missiles at the same time . . .

I shook my head and pulled free from Fi and Mother. The whole room was silent, waiting for me to speak.

'Well?' said Fi. 'Caitlin, what are you waiting for?'

I turned to Mother and sighed.

'If I stay . . . do I have to get a tattoo?'

The rest of the night was a blur. After I agreed to stay and convinced Fi to do the same, Mother said we should celebrate. I stayed up till midnight, but Fi slipped off by herself not long afterwards. I was worried I'd upset her by siding with Mother, but I promised myself I'd make it up to her soon – maybe with some more pasta.

When I opened my eyes the next morning, I knew immediately that something was wrong. I sat up. All of Fi's stuff had gone.

'. . . Fi?'

I searched the entire boat but she was nowhere. When I went out onto the deck I found Mother and the women standing at the edge, gazing across the water.

'Come, child!' said Mother. 'We were just admiring the view.'

The river around us was unrecognisable. The flooding was even worse now. It looked like an ocean, stretching out in every direction as far as the eye could see and dotted with treetops.

'All this extra water has made our journey quicker than expected,' Mother explained. 'We can sail through the next village and that's it – we'll be at the city tomorrow morning!'

All the old ladies cheered. I smiled weakly.

'That's great,' I said. 'But has anyone seen F— I mean, Queenie?' I glanced around. 'I can't find her anywhere. Or her cow.'

There was a heavy silence. Mother placed a hand on my shoulder.

'I'm afraid there is some bad news, child.' She sighed. 'It seems ... well, it seems that your friend climbed overboard last night. She has left us.'

I was stunned.

'N – no,' I said, shaking my head. 'You're wrong. Fi would *never* ...'

'Our lifeboat is missing,' said Mother. 'The women found this lying in the slipway.'

She held out a bobble hat with the words FI QEENY written on the front. I was speechless.

'I am sorry,' said Mother. 'I could tell how much you liked her.'

I couldn't believe it. I couldn't believe Fi would just leave in the middle of the night without even saying goodbye. I mean, Mum or Dad or Frank letting me down was one thing, but Fi ... well, Fi was different.

'I thought she was my friend,' I said.

Mother shook her head. 'No, Caitlin. She was never a true friend – not if she abandoned you when you needed her the most.'

Mother was right. My eyes started stinging really badly.

'Hush, child,' said Mother, holding my face. 'Don't waste your tears on her. She's not worth it.' She took my hand. 'Come – I have something to show you.'

She led me to the edge of the boat. Ahead of us lay a village – at least, the top half of a village. The other half was under water. All the shops had moved up a floor and were selling stuff out the windows with sticks. The high street was filled with rowboats and rubber dinghies, people clattering their oars against lampposts.

'You and I are taking a trip,' Mother explained.

172

'I rarely leave the boat nowadays – but today I will make an exception, for you. There's something in this village I would like you to see.'

I wiped my eyes. 'The others aren't coming with us?'

Mother shook her head. 'They have too much to prepare for tomorrow, my dear. Besides, this is a chance for the two of us to spend some time together before we see Perijee. That's what *real* friends do – isn't it?'

I smiled, and Mother smiled back.

'Now, look sharp!' she said. 'Our bus has arrived.'

A giant raft was floating down the road towards us, made of thousands of empty plastic bottles tied with string. It stopped and a handful of people leapt through the window of the nearest building. A small boy was left standing on top, sunburned and shirtless, holding a rope that stretched down the road behind him.

'Where to?' he said.

The theatre was pretty good, considering it was under water.

It wasn't *all* under water – the stage was flooded, but the balcony seats were high enough to stay dry.

Mother and me sat in our own private box, eating ice creams and watching the spotlights dance on the ripples below.

'Amazing, isn't it?' said Mother. 'I was going to take you to the cinema but apparently it's infested with beavers.'

An usher appeared to take our tickets. At once Mother sank into her chair and bent over double, looking up at him with bleary eyes.

'Ooh, hello, young man!' she croaked, just like a normal old lady. 'Two please – for me and my lovely granddaughter!'

I almost choked on my ice cream but managed to keep a straight face. We waited until the usher had gone before cracking up. It was nice to be happy again.

'I hope you don't mind me saying that,' Mother chuckled.

I frowned. 'Saying what?'

'That you were my granddaughter.'

I didn't mind at all, but I tried not to look too pleased.

Down below, a man in a tuxedo was rowing into the centre of the stage.

'Ladies and gentlemen!' he announced, standing

up and almost tipping the boat over. 'Tonight's performance of *The Tempest* has been cancelled due to bad weather.'

Everyone booed.

'Instead we have a stand-in performance!' He gave a flourish of his arms. 'Presenting ... *The Water Puppeteers of Saigon*!'

All the lights slammed off at once and the room turned black. Mother leaned in close.

'Have you ever seen water puppetry before?' she asked.

I shook my head. 'I've never been to a theatre.'

Mother was shocked.

'Your own mother or father never took you, child?' She snorted. '*Honestly!* These so-called "parents" of yours ... if you ask me, you were smart to leave them behind!'

It felt wrong for her to say it – but the more I thought about it, the more I realised she was right. I'd come all this way without them, hadn't I? And even after Frank and Fi had given up on me, I'd still kept going.

I grinned. They were going to feel so *stupid* when I saved the world all by myself.

A tiny light appeared on the water below. It wasn't

a stage light – it was a candle. A candle held up by a wooden hand.

'What's that?' I whispered.

'Just watch,' said Mother.

The hand started to rise out the water. It kept lifting up, bit by bit, until a wooden arm appeared – and then a whole wooden man, rising up and up until it stood on the surface of the water. There was nothing holding him in place at all. It was like magic.

'But ... how?' I said. 'He doesn't have any strings!'

Mother smiled. 'He doesn't need them, child.'

She pointed to the water. You could just glimpse a metal pole beneath the puppet's feet, moving him up and down.

'The poles are hidden in the water,' said Mother. 'The puppeteers control him from behind the curtain.' She nodded. 'A simple trick – but with an important message. The answer is not always where you expect it to be.'

The puppet started dancing across the stage, spreading ripples wherever he went. Mother watched him, her eyes sparkling.

'I was your age when I left home, Caitlin,' she said. 'I went searching for answers – no, more than that. For *love*. I searched for years – far from my friends and family, far from everyone I had ever known . . . and found nothing.'

The puppet suddenly stopped dead.

'So I gave up,' said Mother. 'I found myself alone in a destroyed temple at the furthest edge of the world. And I promised myself that when I reached the top of the tallest tower, I would throw myself off it.'

The lights in the room began to turn red. The puppet slowly sank back under water.

'That's where I found the Prophecy,' Mother whispered. 'Carved into the walls at the very top. It hadn't been seen in a thousand years. The words had almost crumbled to dust.'

The water on stage started trembling. I shifted in my seat nervously.

'And below them,' said Mother, 'I found something else. *Symbols*.'

The water started to roll and boil across the stage. I felt like something terrible was about to happen – but Mother just kept staring ahead, lost in her story.

'I've devoted my whole life to him, Caitlin,' she said. 'To the creature from the Prophecy. The one who will take us all to a better place.' She turned to me. 'I love him even more than you do. He is my god.'

I frowned. How could Perijee be a *god*? I thought of all the times I'd watched him hold tiny bugs in his hands, and the first time he swam.

'Are you *sure* it's Perijee?' I said. 'I mean, those symbols carved on your door – they're not even the same ones on his body.'

Mother gazed down at me. I could see her trying to make a decision, right at the back of her eyes. Then she leaned forwards and slowly opened her mouth. Soon it lay wide open in the darkness – so wide I could see all the way to the back. I gasped.

'. . . Your teeth,' I whispered.

Every one of them had been carved with symbols. On the inside, where they couldn't be seen – not unless you were right up close. The stage lights glowed through them like lanterns.

'Who did that to you?'

'I did, child.'

A dragon suddenly exploded out of the water on stage. It was a huge puppet, his body held up by a dozen poles that swirled and twisted him through the air. His mouth was filled with fireworks that roared and whistled out of him, bursting across the water in a coil of stars.

'I did it to prove my love,' said Mother. 'My devotion. I did it all for him. I've been waiting to meet him my whole life, Caitlin. It *has* to be him.'

I didn't know what to say.

'But ... didn't it *hurt*?'

Mother smiled. 'It was agony, child.'

There was a sudden scream beside us. The audience were on their feet, pointing at the stage. The dragon had caught fire. He was writhing and swinging his head across the water. Rockets were exploding out his mouth at random, bouncing off the rafters and whizzing over the balcony. Suddenly the puppet had turned to face right where I was sitting ...

'*Get down!*' Mother cried, jumping out of her seat.

... as a rocket flared out his mouth and came roaring across the theatre towards me ...

I covered my head just as the rocket slammed into Mother's back, sending a net of sparks around us. I looked up, my heart pounding. The seats either side of us were on fire. Mother was hunched before me, her back smoking.

'Mother!' I said. 'Are you hurt?'

Before I knew what was happening she had pulled me out of my chair and wrapped her tree-trunk arms around me, so tight I couldn't breathe.

'Oh, my child!' she sobbed. 'I thought I was too late! I thought I'd lost you!'

I didn't stop her – I didn't want to. I'd never been hugged like that. The whole room exploded in smoke and colour around us, but it might as well have been a thousand miles away. It was like nothing mattered in the world except me and Mother.

'My wonderful girl! My star!'

Because – for the first time since Perijee had reached out and taken my hand – I felt like someone really needed me.

The water glistened like foil under the morning sun. There it was, ahead of us – the city.

'What do you think?' said Mother.

I shook my head. 'It . . . it's like another planet.'

The last stretch of the river had been as empty as a desert. But now a maze of chimneys and skyscrapers jutted out of the water ahead of us, each one wrapped in tentacles that slithered up from the city below. It was beautiful.

I wished Fi had been there to see it with me.

'Look, child,' said Mother, pointing past the warships. 'There he is.'

Far ahead of us lay the blockade of warships, linked by metal chains. And beyond them . . . the Monster.

He was more like a mountain now. He stretched across the horizon from end to end, the symbols carved into him maybe fifty storeys high. Huge long tentacles draped down his sides, searching tirelessly through the water around us. His mouth gaped open so wide that the top of his head nearly touched the clouds.

I shaded my eyes from the sun. Somewhere up there was Perijee. But I had no idea how we were going to get to him – let alone past the blockade. He seemed so far away.

'Beautiful, isn't he?'

Mother was gazing ahead with a faint smile on her lips. I was surprised.

'You can see him?' I said. '*I* can't. All I can see up there is that . . . well, it looks like a *house*.'

Mother just smiled.

'Beautiful,' she whispered.

I stared at her in confusion. I realised she wasn't talking about Perijee.

She was talking about the Monster.

'What do you mean?' I said. 'He's *horrible*.'

I glanced at the other old ladies. They all stood in silence behind Mother, gazing at the black mouth on the horizon. Suddenly everything seemed wrong.

'. . . Who's driving the boat?' I said.

The edge of a sunken building swung past us,

missing by inches. I cried out, but the women didn't even flinch. Their eyes were all fixed on the Monster. A ball of fear started growing in my chest. The army blockade was getting closer.

'We have to stop the boat,' I said. 'They're going to see us.'

But the women didn't listen. The boat kept going, pushing past the last of the skyscrapers until there was nothing between us and the warships but open water. I could see the soldiers pointing down at us, and the guns mounted on their decks. I grabbed Mother by the sleeve.

'Why aren't we stopping?' I cried. 'They're going to shoot!'

'At long last,' Mother said calmly, 'the final part of the Prophecy has come to pass.'

All the women bowed their heads. My skin prickled in horror.

'But . . . there's no way we can get past them now,' I said. 'They've seen us.'

Mother looked up at the warships. The soldiers on deck were aiming their guns at us. But Mother wasn't frightened. She was *smiling*.

'They were going to kill him, Caitlin,' she said. 'I want you to remember that.'

Her voice sounded different – like a stranger. I let go of her sleeve.

'Remember wh—'

BOOM.

The warship ahead exploded like a sun – then the next one along, and the next, and the next. The sound was so loud it was like being in a different world. A wall of air threw me back across the deck and smashed me into a door.

The last thing I saw before everything turned black was Mother's shadow as explosion after explosion tore through the army blockade behind it – like it was cut out of fire.

'Careful with her.'

My ears were ringing.

'Quick.'

I opened my eyes. I was being carried to the front of the boat. The warships lay in a ring of twisted metal behind us, pouring black smoke into the sky. There was fire everywhere you looked.

'I'm sorry, child,' came Mother's voice. 'I know you asked for no one to be hurt.'

She stood calmly beside me, her gaze fixed on the horizon. The boat was ploughing through the water at top speed, thundering over the tentacles.

'But we could not risk them stopping us,' she said. 'Not now we're so close.'

The truth hit me like a belt across the face.

'No,' I whispered.

Mother had blown up the ships. She had only taken me to the theatre so the bombs could be planted without me knowing. She had been lying to me all along.

'You see, Caitlin,' said Mother, 'there is *so* much about the Prophecy I didn't tell you.'

Both my wrists suddenly stung with pain. Two women were tying my hands hard to the railings.

'It says a powerful creature will lead us to paradise,' said Mother. 'But it is the *Monster* who holds the power. Perijee is simply one stage in his life: the child before the man. And now it is time for his final transformation.'

I pulled desperately at the ropes. 'Fi was right about you – you're mad! Let me go!'

Mother shook her head. 'I'm afraid I can't do that, Caitlin. We must begin the last stage of the Prophecy, before the army sends its planes.'

The women knelt on deck and closed their eyes.

The Monster's mouth lay ahead of us, his fifty rows of teeth towering up like a tidal wave.

'The last stage,' said Mother. 'When he finally becomes a god. When he destroys this world and makes a new one in its place – a paradise right here on Earth.' She sighed. 'But he cannot do it on his own, Caitlin. No – he needs a gift first. A *special* gift.'

She reached over and held my face.

'He needs a sacrifice.'

Her words were like needles being pushed through my skin.

'No,' I whispered. 'You . . . you can't!'

Mother nodded. '*Love*, Caitlin. I could see it in you the first time we met – pure, perfect love for Perijee.' She gazed up at the Monster. 'You will be the greatest gift I could ever offer him.'

The inside of the Monster's mouth finally came into view. It was like a cathedral.

'If you can kill the thing you love . . .' said Mother. 'Well, you can do anything, can't you?'

The top of the Monster's mouth appeared overhead, cutting across the sun. I heaved and pulled against the ropes, but it was no use – I was stuck fast. Darkness began to close around us.

'Please,' I begged, 'just let me go! I won't tell anyone about what you've done – I'll take Perijee and you can have the Monster all to yourself, I won't try to stop you . . .'

'No, Caitlin,' said Mother, shaking her head. 'It's too late for that now. The final stage has already begun.'

The Monster's throat emerged from the darkness in front of us. I screamed. It was a long, deep tunnel made of twisting fangs. Mother rested her hands gently on my shoulders.

'It will be over so quickly, child,' she said. 'Don't fight it.'

There was a noise, like the first rumble of thunder. The air began to turn hot and damp around us.

And then the teeth began to move.

'Don't be afraid,' said Mother.

And all of a sudden, the strangest thing happened. I *wasn't* afraid.

When you know you're about to die, you can think clearly again. I realised how sorry I was for leaving Mum and Frank behind. I realised I should have believed in Fi. And more than anything, I realised that I didn't want to spend the last moment of my life screaming and crying in the darkness.

So instead I closed my eyes and I thought about the most wonderful thing I could think of.

I thought about Perijee.

BAM.

The hit was so sudden that for a second I thought, *that's it – I'm dead.* But when I opened my eyes, I saw that the darkness had gone. We weren't even in the mouth any more. We'd been knocked back outside. The boat was spinning around in circles and Mother was reeling beside me.

'*WHAT WAS—*'

CRUNCH.

Something hit the deck, splintering the wood. It was an anchor.

I looked across the water. Another boat had appeared out of nowhere and driven straight into us, and was now dragging us towards itself like a fish on a line. A man stood at the front. He had a beard and a paunch, and he had his hands on his hips like a rubbish action figure.

'*Frank!*'

He gave me a nod.

'All right, sprat.'

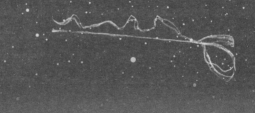

Frank looked like he'd been living on a boat for days. His beard was longer and his trousers were even more stained than usual, but it was him.

And standing right beside him . . .

'*Fi!*' I cried.

'Oh, don't look so surprised,' she muttered.

She reeled in the anchor and the two boats crashed into each other. Frank leapt onto the deck and started cutting at my ropes. Mother and the old ladies were too horrified to try to stop him.

'WHAT ... WHAT HAVE YOU DONE?' Mother bellowed, shaking with rage. 'YOU HAVE *DESTROYED* THE FINAL COMING OF THE—'

'Sod off,' said Frank firmly. 'I'm taking Caitlin and there's nothing you can do about it.'

Mother stopped. A horrible smile spread across her face.

'Oh, really?' she said. 'Is that so?'

She gave a nod to the women beside her. They immediately stepped forwards, cracking their knuckles. Frank rolled his eyes.

'Oh, come off it – if you think I'm going to lay a finger on some old biddy, then you're ...'

Without a word the women swooped on top of him, shrieking and pummelling him to the ground.

'*No!*' I screamed. *'FRANK ... !'*

I stopped. Actually, Frank was doing OK. He was fighting back – and I mean, *really* fighting back. He might have had problems with laying a finger on old ladies, but he didn't seem to have any problems with laying a foot on them, or a fist, or with tombstoning them, or with throwing them overboard like frisbees.

'Wow, Frank!' I said. 'Look at you go!'

'Shut up and help me,' he shouted, wrestling Margaret into a headlock.

Suddenly Fi was beside me too, frantically hacking away at the ropes.

'Fi!' I cried. 'I can't believe it – you came back!'

She snorted. 'I never *left*, Caitlin. I was behind you the whole time! I could sense those women were up to something the moment we stepped on board – but when they confessed to being Obsidian Blade, I knew I wouldn't last the night. I got out as quick as I could and went back to Wanderly for a proper boat – and found *that* one looking for you when I got there.'

She nodded at Frank, who was swinging an old lady round his head by her ankles.

'It's been interesting,' said Fi, breaking the last rope. 'Now, come on! We've got to get out of here, before the planes—'

A hand slammed over her mouth.

'STOP OR SHE DIES.'

Everyone swung around. Mother was clutching Fi against her chest, a knife pressed to her neck.

'I mean it,' said Mother, glaring at me. 'Lie on the floor right now or I'll cut her throat.'

I looked at the knife and Fi and Frank. There was nothing I could do. The boat was spinning around in circles. There was no way out without Fi getting hurt. We were trapped . . .

. . . And then I saw it.

'Frank, give up!' I said quickly. 'Just do what she says!'

Frank opened his mouth to argue, and then he saw what I'd seen. Without another word he threw himself to the ground and covered his head. Mother laughed and shoved Fi towards me.

'*That*,' she said, 'was a very stupid thing to do.'

I grinned. 'You're telling me.'

I hit the ground and took Fi with me.

BAM.

The boat smashed into the Monster's teeth at full speed, so hard that they ripped clean through the hull. Mother flew back, her feet stumbling, her arms pinwheeling . . .

'*NO!*' she cried.

She managed two more steps before pitching overboard and hitting the sea like a meteor dropped from the sky. I leapt to my feet – there was no time to lose. The anchor holding the two boats together had almost pulled free. The deck was being prised apart beneath us like chicken bones.

'*Jump!*' I shouted, grabbing Frank and Fi. '*Now!*'

We leapt through the air and into Frank's boat just as the anchor ripped through the deck and sent us careering across the water. Frank grabbed the wheel.

'Look back, Caitlin!' he shouted. 'Are they following us?'

I spun round, my heart pounding. There was no way the other boat could follow us now – what hadn't been torn to pieces against the Monster's teeth was sinking fast. The old women were floundering into the water, their nightgowns billowing around them like jellyfish.

'No, they're not!' I said. 'We made it! They're all ...'

I stopped. Someone was heaving herself up onto the Monster's teeth behind us, stumbling to her feet.

'*No ... no, please!*'

It was Mother. I could only just hear her over the noise of the engine.

'*Come back! Don't go, please! Don't leave me!*'

She was crying like a child, holding her arms out across the water – like she could pick me up and take me back somehow. She didn't look so frightening any more.

The boat kept going. I watched as Mother got smaller and smaller, until she was so far away that I couldn't see her any more, until the water had covered her completely.

Frank shut the motor off and threw the anchor into a tentacle beside us. It landed with a *splut*.

'You all right?' he muttered.

I nodded. 'Yeah. I'm OK.'

Frank smiled. For a moment everything was quiet. But only for a moment.

'*WHAT WERE YOU THINKING?! Running away like that without saying anything, with NO clue where you were, I mean, honest to god, I had to just sit there and think the WORST, IF YOU HAD ANY IDEA WHAT I'VE GONE THROUGH …*'

Frank finally took a breath.

'I mean, if I hadn't remembered what you'd said about going to that meeting in Wanderly …'

I gasped. 'You were at the meeting too?'

'Course I was!' said Frank. 'I got there as fast as I could! But I couldn't find you anywhere – I searched all round the town, but nothing. And after the theatre got blown up . . . well, that was just terrible. I thought you were dead, sprat. I thought I was going to have to go back to the camp and tell your mum that I was too late . . .'

My chest ached the moment he said it. Mum must have been so worried. After all, she'd done everything she did to try and keep me safe. I couldn't believe I'd just run away without telling her.

'Is she . . . OK?' I said nervously.

'No!' said Frank. 'She's been going out of her mind, Caitlin! We all were! I mean, if I hadn't bumped into your friend in Wanderly, running around with a cow and talking about you being kidnapped . . .'

He nodded to Fi, sat on the gutbox beside me.

'She's something, that one,' Frank muttered. I couldn't tell if it was a compliment or not. 'Bought this boat herself, you know – out her own pocket.'

I swung round. 'Fi! You didn't!'

Fi blushed.

'But . . . where'd you get the money from?' I said.

'Where do you think?' said Frank. 'She had a *cow*, Caitlin! They're just about the most valuable thing in the world right now. You should have seen what people were offering her for it – someone tried to sell her Westminster Abbey.'

'So *that's* why you stole it,' I muttered.

'She spent it all on this boat,' said Frank. 'Every penny. I would have helped pay for it too, but someone at the meeting stole my wallet.'

Fi blushed even more.

'Er . . . let's get going, shall we?' she said. 'The sooner we get away from here, the better.'

Frank turned to the wheel. But before he could start the engine I grabbed his hand.

'No,' I said. 'We're not going. Not without Perijee.'

Fi and Frank shared a worried look.

'Caitlin,' said Fi. 'Look, I know you want to help him . . . but come on, don't be *stupid* . . .'

'I'm not stupid,' I said. 'I've travelled the whole country to get here. I've been kidnapped and lied to and nearly sacrificed and I could have given up any time, but I didn't. I'm not leaving here without him.'

Frank stepped forwards.

'Sprat,' he said gently. 'The army could get here any second. If you're on top of that thing when they do . . .'

'Perijee's my friend,' I said. 'My brother. If I was stuck up there and the army was coming, would you go without me?'

Frank and Fi shook their heads.

'Of course not,' I said. I put my hands on my hips. 'And neither am I.'

Fi jumped off the gutbox.

'Fine! We'll climb on top of the Monster and hope being super nice to him fixes everything. But the *second* it doesn't work . . .'

She trailed off. She read my face quickly – she was good at it now.

'Oh god,' she said. 'You want to go by yourself, don't you?'

I nodded. 'I'm the only one who can fix this, Fi.'

She considered arguing with me some more, but gave up. That's what I loved most about Fi – she always knew when I meant it.

'Honestly, Caitlin,' she grumbled. 'I've *never* had a friend like you before.'

She turned around and pulled Frank's hands off the wheel.

'Well, you heard her! She's going to get Perijee!' She took out the keys and sat down on them. 'We're not going *anywhere* till she's done.'

Frank gave Fi the sort of look you'd give a small, savage cat that occasionally let you feed it.

'All right, sprat,' he muttered. 'We'll take you to the Monster's side and wait until you're done.' He wagged a finger at me. 'But the *second* you see those planes ...'

I didn't even let him finish. I ran over and gave them both the biggest hug you've ever seen.

'Frank – Fi,' I said. 'I don't care what everyone else says about you. You are both the absolute best.'

We hugged. For a moment everything was perfect.

Then Frank pulled away. He looked like he'd finally worked something out.

'Hang on a minute – "Fi"? You told me your name was Queenie!'

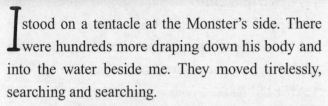

I stood on a tentacle at the Monster's side. There were hundreds more draping down his body and into the water beside me. They moved tirelessly, searching and searching.

A giant symbol lay ahead, carved a metre deep into the Monster's body. It ran all the way up to his back, so high I couldn't even see where it ended. I recognised it from when Perijee was small: two vertical lines, criss-crossed like teeth, tucked in the space beneath his shoulder.

I still had no idea what it meant. But that didn't matter right now.

I grabbed one of the horizontal lines. It squidged softly in my hand. I heaved myself up and stood on it. It bent like warm rubber under my feet – but it held.

Just like a ladder.

I climbed the giant symbol, until the boat was

just a speck in the water below. It felt like hours until I finally heaved myself onto the Monster's back, gasping for breath. The midday sun beat off his skin so brightly that it burned my eyes.

'Hello!' said a voice.

I looked up, squinting. There was a man standing in front of me.

'Welcome aboard!' he said. 'Let me guess – End of the World Appreciation Club?'

My eyes finally focused on him. He was wearing yellow wellies and a blue bobble hat. The hat said 'CAITLIN' on it.

'Well, good to see you're wearing the correct robes,' he said, nodding at my clothes. 'Most of the others have to make their own before they're allowed to see the Master – but you can join them straight away!'

He pointed behind him. Far in the distance, a massive procession was making its way across the Monster's back towards the head – hundreds and hundreds of people, all wearing hats and wellies. I was so confused I didn't know what question to ask first.

'Wh-where are they going?' I said.

The man smiled. 'To the Temple, of course. To

see the Master.'

He turned to the Monster's head and bowed. I blinked against the sun. There in the distance, right where Perijee should have been, was a huge white building. I stared at it in disbelief.

'Amazing, isn't it?' said the man. 'The Master built it all himself. We brought him the materials, of course, but everything else was his idea. After all, he needs somewhere to store all those books he reads.'

It took me a while to work out exactly what I was looking at – I guess at first I couldn't believe my eyes. But it looked like I'd been right all along. There *was* a house on top of the Monster's head.

It was *my* house.

By the time I reached the front door there was already a huge crowd outside, kneeling and chanting in wellies and bobble hats. All their hats said 'CAITLIN' on the front.

The house looked exactly like our one on Middle Island, in every way. The bricks, the doors – all the same. The only difference was that it was bright white. And the windows . . .

I reached out and touched one. It was just a picture, drawn on the wall.

'*Get back!*'

A gang of men in hats and wellies were standing at the front door, trying to push everyone away.

'The Master is angry!' one of them announced. 'He doesn't want any more visitors – he wants everyone to leave!'

Everyone booed and started trying to barge forwards. It was all the men could do to hold them back. No one noticed me as I slipped between their legs and edged my way along the wall, silently stepping through the front door and closing it behind me.

The inside of the house was identical too. I looked into the study. The same broken lightbulb hung from the same dusty lampshade. An unfinished cup of tea sat on the desk. And behind it, scribbled on the wall . . .

My heart glowed.

'Mum.'

It wasn't really her, of course. It was just a drawing. But whoever drew her had remembered her perfectly. Her eyes. Her haircut. The jumper she wore round the house.

I reached out and touched it. Suddenly I would have given anything to be back home, just me and her, the way it was. I couldn't believe I had ever wanted anything different.

'*Master, please ... !*'

The shouts came from the kitchen. I looked at the closed door. There in front of it was the same rug with the same burned corner; the same wooden chest with the same crayon stains on the side. Perijee had remembered everything.

'*Master, we beg you! Stop!*'

There was the sound of glasses breaking and cupboards being torn off walls. I walked to the kitchen door and stood in the darkness in front of it. The walls around me were covered with symbols – just like the ones on Perijee's body. They spread across the floor and onto the ceiling like an oil slick. There were so many that the door looked like it had been painted black.

Except for one patch.

I ran my fingers over the drawing. There I was – in yellow wellies and a bobble hat with 'CAITLIN' on the front. The me he remembered.

I pushed open the door and stepped inside.

The kitchen was different to the rest of the house. It was ten times bigger than it should have been, warped and magnified out of all proportion. You couldn't tell from outside – everything looked normal there. But here, the walls stretched up so high you could barely make out the ceiling. Each black and white floor tile was the size of a stage, and every surface was covered in scribbled symbols and stacks of tumbling books.

And in the middle of it was Perijee.

He was still sunk waist-deep in the Monster's head. But he was ten times bigger now. His body sprouted up from the floor like a tree, all the way to the ceiling. He had hundreds of arms too, and he was ripping the kitchen apart with every single one of them, tearing cupboards from the wall and shredding the books to sawdust.

'There is no need to lose hope, Master!' came a voice from the corner. 'There is still time!'

A handful of terrified men and women in blue hats and yellow wellies were cowering beside the enormous stove like mice. One of them stepped forwards.

'You ... you are sure to solve the symbols *somehow*!' the man said. 'We have more followers than ever before – they will do anything you ask, Master! They *love* you!'

Perijee stopped. He started trembling. His whole body was turning red.

'Perhaps – perhaps the Master would like some

more books?' the man suggested nervously. 'Before the planes get here . . . ?'

Perijee swung round. In a flash he grew twenty more arms and grabbed the man from the ground, lifting him high into the air.

'Master – no!' said the man. 'What are you doing? Stop!'

But Perijee didn't stop. He squeezed the man in front of him like a fruit, his grip getting tighter and tighter. His face had turned hard and mean, and his mouth was curling into a smile . . .

'*PERIJEE, NO!*' I cried.

Perijee swung round, dropping the man in surprise.

'What are you doing?' I said. 'You'll hurt him!'

Perijee was too shocked to move – he didn't even answer me. At once, the people in the corner flew across the room.

'*Lower your voice when talking to the Master . . . !*'
'*Entrance to the Temple is forbidden . . . !*'
'*Out at once . . . !*'

Perijee shot out an arm and in one sweep of his giant hand threw them all back.

The kitchen was silent now. Perijee stood still, his eyes fixed on me and his chest rising and falling.

The colour of his skin slowly drained white.

Then – like a plant – his body bent over and his head came down to my level. He pointed outside with a shaking hand, to the drawing in the darkness.

'. . . Caitlin?' he said.

His voice was so quiet I could barely hear it. I smiled.

'Yes, Perijee. It's me. I came to get you.'

I reached out and touched his face. It was exactly as I remembered it. The candle softness of his skin; the bobble hat; his tiny, sad, dark eyes. The only thing missing was his smile.

'Oh, Perijee,' I said. 'What happened to you?'

Perijee said nothing. I looked around the room, covered in symbols that made no sense, stacked high with heaps of useless books.

'You . . . you've been trying to work out what the symbols mean,' I said. 'You thought they might tell you how to turn back – how to fix everything.'

Perijee nodded.

'And you still don't know?' I said.

Perijee shook his head. He looked so sad. Suddenly his eyes turned a colour I'd never seen before. His cheeks and throat and chest turned grey, getting darker and darker. Before I knew what was happening he put his head in his hands and gave a cry that was so miserable and lost I thought I was going to cry myself just listening to it. I held him tight.

'Don't be sad, Perijee,' I said. 'I know how to fix everything! It's all going to go back to the way it was! You and me – together again! We'll get you away from here and go back to Middle Island and work out what to do . . .'

I looked around the room.

'This house – the kitchen – it's so perfect, Perijee. How did you do it?'

Perijee smiled. He held his arms out to the room.

'Home,' he said.

The kitchen door slammed open. A man was standing in the doorway in a hat and wellies, his face white with fear.

'*The planes!*' he cried. '*They're coming!*'

I swung round to the window and my stomach dropped. Hundreds of planes were coming towards us, blackening the sky. Perijee stared at them in horror, his whole body turning purple. I grabbed him by the arm and pulled him closer.

'No – don't be frightened, Perijee!' I said. 'We can still fix it!'

'No we can't!' said the man in the corner, ripping

off his hat. 'I'm getting out of here!'

He turned and fled. The others followed him without a moment's thought, throwing off their hats and wellies as they went. Suddenly it was just me and Perijee. I held his head and looked deep into his eyes.

'Listen to me, Perijee,' I said. 'Remember the first time you changed? It was because you were frightened. You have to forget about everything that's upsetting you, Perijee. You have to be happy.'

The planes were getting closer. Perijee tried to turn to the window but I pulled his head back.

'No!' I said. 'Think about something nice. We both have to do it.'

I took his hands in mine and closed my eyes. I thought about Frank and Fi and how much I loved them. I thought about seeing Mum again. I thought about the days Perijee and me spent together on the island, just the two of us.

'One two three,' I said. 'Remember that, Perijee? The first thing I ever taught you.'

Perijee looked at me. His smile came back.

'One two three,' he said.

I beamed. 'That's it, Perijee! And the other things – remember the day I took your photo on the beach?'

I reached into my pocket and pulled out the photo. It was even more stained and crumpled now, but there we were in the middle, our arms around each other. Perijee held it in front of him and glowed right up to the bobble on his hat.

'Family,' he said. 'Friends.'

Something was happening. The floor beneath us was trembling. Plates and glasses were falling out the kitchen cupboards and smashing on the floor. I held his hands.

'You're doing it, Perijee!' I said. 'You're shrinking! Keep going – think about the happiest thing you know.'

Perijee's body burned so bright it nearly blinded me. He grew a hundred hands and a thousand fingers, and he wrapped them all around me.

'Caitlin,' he said.

And just like that, everything changed.

The whole room was falling apart around us. Smashed plates and cupboards were flying across the floor, piling against the walls. The Monster's head was lifting up out of the water.

'Perijee . . . what's going on?' I shouted. 'Are *you* doing this?'

Perijee said nothing. His eyes were fixed out the window, the symbols on his body burning brighter than ever. The Monster's head had lifted so high it was almost vertical, sticking out the water like a rocket. Through the window I could see hundreds of people toppling off his back and plummeting to the sea in a flurry of hats and wellies. If Perijee hadn't been holding on to me I would have fallen too.

'Why isn't he shrinking?' I cried. 'Perijee, why—'

In one great explosion the Monster burst up from the water and all the breath was knocked out of me.

The city shrank behind us and the planes disappeared in an instant. The walls of the kitchen trembled and shook and the windows creaked and splintered with the strain . . .

And then the wind pulled the roof from over our heads and the walls were prised apart and there was nothing around us but sky.

We were flying!

The Monster tore through the air like a firework. I clung on to Perijee for dear life, but we didn't stop – we just got faster and faster. Suddenly clouds were streaming past us and the wind cut at my face like knives, and I realised with horror that my hands were slipping . . .

'Perijee, help!'

. . . And then it stopped, just like that. The wind disappeared and the roar became a hush.

I opened my eyes. Perijee had wrapped his hands around me – but he'd changed them. Now they were big as boat sails and as clear as glass. It was like sitting inside a bubble. And outside it . . .

'Oh wow,' I whispered.

We were above the clouds. A world of white stretched out endlessly beside us. The Monster flew and dipped and twisted like a ribbon in the wind, the rest of his body forming a great rainbow road in the sky behind us. There was nothing holding him up at all. It was like magic.

'But – I don't understand,' I said. 'Wasn't the Monster supposed to disappear?'

I looked up at Perijee, and I was surprised by what I saw. He suddenly looked ... different. Like something behind his eyes had changed.

He knew what was happening.

'Perijee,' I said. 'Do you know where he's taking us?'

Perijee smiled. He took my hand and placed it over one of the symbols on his chest. It was glowing harder than all the others combined, throbbing and fading like a nightlight.

'Home,' he said.

I gasped.

'The Monster's taking us home – back to Middle Island? *That's* what that symbol means?'

Perijee shook his head. I didn't understand at first – but then it hit me. My face fell.

'Oh crumbs,' I said. 'You mean ... he's taking you to *your* home?'

Perijee nodded, smile after smile appearing on his face and floating across his skin. I gulped.

'Oh,' I said. 'I've never been into space before. I wish I'd brought a thicker jumper or ...'

I stopped. Clouds were streaming past us again.

'We're falling,' I said.

We were getting faster and faster. The Monster was plummeting back to the sea, spinning and diving like a flock of birds. Suddenly he made a great dipping arc like a rollercoaster through the sky and reeled to one side. The rest of his body followed, until we'd formed an enormous spiral above the sea.

'What's he *doing*?' I shouted.

We were in the middle of nowhere, high above the ocean. It was just me and Perijee and nothing else for miles and miles. You could just make out the moon in the sky above us, fading into place like it had never gone away. I looked up at Perijee, confused.

'I ... I thought you just said you were going home,' I said. 'What are we doing down here?'

Perijee said nothing. He was gazing down at the water, his face covered in smiles, the symbols on his body still glowing. The Monster's tail was lowering to the sea, his tentacles twisting their way after it.

'Wait – what's going on?' I cried.

The Monster started spinning in the air. Bit by bit

his great body was coiling down into the water and disappearing under the waves.

'Perijee ... he's sinking!' I said. 'He's going to drag you down with him! We have to get you free!'

Perijee didn't seem to understand. He was still smiling. I grabbed his head.

'Perijee, *listen to me*,' I said. 'If you go under too, you'll drown. Things like us ... we can't *breathe* under water.'

The Monster kept on sinking. It was only a matter of time before his head reached the water. But Perijee just kept smiling.

'Aren't you listening to me, Perijee?' I said. 'You're supposed to be going *home* ...'

There it was again – the change in his eyes. They were so clear all of a sudden. He had never looked happier.

And suddenly it clicked.

I looked down at the Monster's body beneath us as it twisted into the black sea. Then I looked up at Perijee.

'... *That's* home?' I said quietly. 'Down there?'

Perijee glowed in my arms. The symbol on his chest burned brighter than ever. I could feel its warmth against me.

'But … but I thought you were an alien,' I said. 'From space.'

Perijee shook his head. He pointed down.

'Mariana Trench,' he said.

I looked down at the Monster as it snaked into the deep, hundreds and hundreds of tentacles winding into the darkness.

'So *that's* why you were so good at swimming,' I said, amazed.

The Monster's head had reached the water now. It plunged into the foam and the waves, and with a great burst of air the mouth sank from sight. Perijee shrank his hands back to normal size and held on to me tight. We stretched over the ocean like a lighthouse, slowly being swallowed into the sea.

'It's getting closer,' I said nervously. 'Are you sure you can breathe under water?'

Perijee nodded. I saw how certain he was. How much it finally made sense to him.

'But … I *can't*, Perijee,' I said.

Perijee kept sinking. The last of the house he had built touched the sea below and scattered across the waves. There was something terrible in the air between us – something neither of us wanted to say.

'That means I can't go with you,' I said.

Perijee's smile vanished. His whole body suddenly felt cold against me. The Monster kept pulling him down. The water was getting closer and closer.

'You can't just … *go*,' I said quietly. 'I came all this way to get you. I'll never see you again.'

Perijee nodded, but his face had turned grey. He was up to his chest in the water now. He carefully placed me on the last of the giant floor tiles that floated on the waves beside us.

'I am sorry,' he said.

Perijee let me go, hand by hand, and I realised how tightly he'd been holding on to me.

And suddenly I couldn't let him go.

'Perijee, wait!'

I grabbed his hand and held it tight as he kept sinking.

'Caitlin…'

'Promise you won't forget about me,' I said. 'I never stopped thinking about you the whole time we were apart. And even though you were miles away, even though I couldn't see you … it was like you were still there. So if we both keep thinking about each other, then we'll always be together. No matter how far apart we are.'

His head was almost touching the water. I kept holding on, clutching the hand to my chest as he stretched further and further away from me.

'Please, Perijee,' I begged. 'You're the best friend I've ever had. You're my brother. Remember me. Please.'

Perijee smiled and looked up at me. He was changing again. Something was appearing in the place above his eyes – a new set of symbols, glowing across his skin where the bottom of his hat would be.

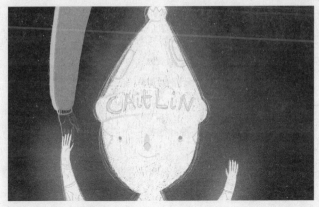

'Promise,' he said.

His head reached the water and I let him go. I watched as he sank down into the deep. The symbols on his body shone brighter than ever, until he was just a white shape in the darkness, a star at nighttime. He waved up at me, and I waved back. He looked so happy. He wasn't lost any more.

The lights on his body faded, one by one. Soon he was barely there, and then he wasn't there at all, and then he was gone.

I sat back on the giant white floor tile. There was nothing around me now but the first of the evening stars, sparkling on the waves, so bright you couldn't tell where the sky ended and the sea began. I had never been so alone in my whole life.

But I didn't *feel* alone. Not any more. My whole body glowed where Perijee had held me. The stars were like a whole other world above me, and the moon had never been closer.

And right there, its reflection glimmering on the water where Perijee had been . . .

'Sirius!'

It wasn't until the Japanese fishing boat picked me up the next morning that I realised how far I was from home.

I told the fishermen my name, and about what had happened, but that was obviously pointless because they didn't speak English. I figured if I kept talking lots they might eventually work out what I was saying. They didn't, but they *did* give me my own Japanese name and wrote it on a sign to wear around my neck! How cool is that? It looked like this:

迷惑な女の子

Then when we got back to land, they couldn't have been more helpful! I suggested that I stay with them for one more day, to sleep, but instead they drove me straight to the embassy and dumped me at the doors and drove off as fast as they could. They didn't even want thanking!

The rest of the journey home was even better. When the embassy worked out who I was, everything changed. They put me in an amazing hotel room all by myself, with a Jacuzzi and a massive TV. It was brilliant, obviously, but to be honest it just reminded me of when Mum said we could go to the Hilton together, and that made me really miss her.

I couldn't wait to see her again. I hoped she wasn't *too* angry with me. She'd probably want to have a good shout and wave her arms a bit, but I figured that was fair enough.

After a few days, the embassy organised a private plane to take me back home – all the normal ones had been grounded after the Monster attack. *That* meant I was the only passenger on the flight, which meant I could lie down across five seats if I wanted to. And I did. The stewardess said if I needed anything then all I had to do was ask! So I asked for a Scotch on the rocks, and she said no.

We finally got back to the city, and as we flew over I couldn't believe how different it looked. Now that the Monster had gone, all the water had drained away – but it had taken everything else with it. There were trees sticking out of buildings, and a tank on the clock tower, and whole streets covered in sand. There were sheep grazing on the runway when we landed.

And then when I stepped out of the plane, I got the biggest shock of all. There were *hundreds* of reporters and people with cameras waiting for me! They all went mad the second they saw me – waving posters with my face on them, and taking my picture, and asking me questions about the Monster and how I knew him.

But then I heard someone shouting over them, really loud. I turned around, and there she was at the front of the crowd.

'. . . Mum?'

'CAITLIN!'

She looked insane. Her hair was all over the place and her eyes were mad and her clothes were torn. I'd never seen her look at me like that before.

She leapt over the barrier to get to me. A soldier tried to stop her but she kicked him right in the nuts and kept running to me. I thought, *Oh, this is it, I'm in trouble now* . . . but then she fell to her knees and grabbed me tight against her so hard it was like she was trying to pull me into her. Everyone was cheering and clapping and taking pictures, but for a moment it was just the two of us. I couldn't believe how much she was crying.

'Oh Caitlin,' she said quietly. 'My wonderful girl.'

And then it didn't matter where I was, because I was home already.

We couldn't go back to Middle Island straight away. First of all lots of people in suits had to ask me questions about Perijee, and where he had come from and where he'd gone and how I'd found him. I gave them really good, extra-long answers, but for some reason this seemed to annoy them so eventually they let me go.

Then, of course, there was the big interview.

I sat in the visitors' section of the dark studio and watched as the cameras turned on and the music started. The newsreader looked up.

'Good evening,' he said. 'This is the news.'

It was the exact same presenter I'd seen talking to Dad just days ago – only since then he'd had his hair cut and dyed into a giant green Mohican.

'Well, it's been exactly one week since everyone thought it was the end of the world and made, er … some bad choices,' he said, trying to flatten the Mohican and failing. 'But we are still left with *hundreds* of unanswered questions about the Monster: who was he? Why did he disappear? And of course: *will he ever come back?*'

(On the screen behind him they played a shot of the ocean where I'd last seen Perijee, filled with boats and helicopters scanning the waves.)

'Perhaps the strangest thing about the Monster is how little we still know about him,' the newsreader continued. 'In particular, where he came from. After a number of *wildly incorrect* theories about him arriving from space on a meteor have left *some people's* reputations in tatters . . .'

(Cut to a shot of Dad's convertible being publicly pelted with his own books.)

'. . . and the members of the violent cults worshipping him have been locked away for good . . .'

(Cut to Mother and dozens of other soaking wet old ladies being piled into police vans, spitting at police officers.)

'. . . we have to accept that the Monster might have come from somewhere else entirely. Here to discuss it with us is the leading world expert on deep-sea marine life: Dr Emily Williams.'

There was Mum, sat beside him. She was a bit

nervous but she looked amazing. I'd never been more proud.

'Go Mum!' I cheered.

After the security guards had got me to stop cheering, they continued with the interview.

'Dr Williams,' said the newsreader, 'perhaps *you* can tell us where the Monster came from?'

Mum coughed lightly.

'Well, to be perfectly frank – no, I can't,' she said. 'Because we still don't know for certain. We *do* know that he comes from somewhere within the Mariana Trench – the deepest, most unexplored part of the world. The part we know the least about.'

The newsreader nodded. 'So why did he come to the surface?'

'Well, he first appeared after the meteor showers,' Mum explained. 'These caused extremely strong storms all across the world. So strong, perhaps, that they swept the Monster up from the bottom of the ocean floor and onto land by accident.'

The newsreader frowned. 'But then ... why did he wait so long to go back?'

Mum shrugged. 'Well, perhaps that's what those tentacles were searching for – a way back home. Maybe he could only go back when the time was right, or when the moon was causing the tides to fall in a certain pattern ... who knows? We think that when one of his tentacles finally found the Trench, the rest of him just followed by instinct.'

I shifted on my chair. I had no idea if what Mum said was right or not. I was there when the Monster took Perijee home – it happened when he became happy again. Of course, it could have been a coincidence ... like how Mother thought Perijee was the creature from the Prophecy, and he wasn't – unless he *was*, of course, and the Prophecy hasn't finished yet ...

I shook my head. There was no point asking those kinds of questions right now. I looked at Mum, who was happier than I had ever seen her, and none of them seemed to matter.

'So what you're saying, Dr Williams,' said the newsreader, leaning forwards, 'is that we might not really know what there is on our own *planet*?'

Mum sighed.

'There's always *something* we don't know anything about,' she said. 'More than we like to admit. The more we discover, the more we realise we don't fully understand. Our world, our solar system, the universe ... It all adds up. I mean, when you think about it – do we even know that much about *ourselves*?'

After her interview, Mum was probably more famous than the Queen. The next day she had calls and letters from universities all over the world, wanting her to start researching again. They even wanted her to go back to the Mariana Trench and lead the investigation into Perijee.

Mum said she'd get back to them, and put the phone down. Then we went out and spent the day together – just the two of us.

They put me and Mum on a train heading back home. Not just any train – we had our own carriage, with beds and a kitchen and everything! It turns out that when you become friends with an alien that tries to take over the world, everyone's really nice to you.

The next morning I walked into our private dining carriage, and there was someone else sitting at the table. I couldn't believe my eyes.

'*Frank!*' I cried.

'All right, sprat!'

He was looking really good – wearing shoes and everything. I gave him a hug.

'What are you doing here?'

'Your mum invited me!' He gave her a sheepish look. 'Which was very kind of her, seeing as, er ... seeing as I'm not her favourite person at the moment.'

Mum gave Frank a dark look.

'He's not?' I said.

'Well, no, Caitlin,' said Mum. 'He put your life in danger. He let you climb onto an alien's back and get carried to the other side of the world.'

'He wasn't an *alien*,' I pointed out. 'Remember? He was a "subterranean megabeast".'

'Whatever,' said Mum. 'Either way, Frank's lucky I haven't killed him.'

She scowled at him again, then smiled.

'That said, if he hadn't gone after you like he did ...'

Frank shrugged, but couldn't hide how much he was blushing. I looked at them both, confused. She was angry, but she wasn't. Adults never make any sense.

'So ... what *are* you doing here?' I asked Frank.

Frank coughed. 'Your mum said something about a plan, sprat. Something she wants to talk to both of us about.'

We looked at Mum expectantly. She shuffled on her chair.

'Er ... yes,' she said. 'But before I get into all that, first of all I should say ... well, even though you should *never* run away like that again, Caitlin, and if I ever find you trying to raise another alien ...'

'Subterranean megabeast,' I corrected.

'Yes, well.' Mum sighed. 'What I'm trying to say is ... I know I'm not free from blame for what happened.' She held my hand. 'I mean, if I'd actually *listened* to you, Caitlin – if I'd spent more time with you on the island, known you a bit better, understood how unhappy you were at school, how lonely you were, and how much Perijee meant to you ... maybe none of this would have happened. At the time I was too sad to see what was wrong with everything ... but that doesn't make it OK. I'm so sorry, Caitlin. I really am.'

She gave my hand a squeeze. I smiled.

'It's fine, Mum.' I meant it, too.

'No it's not,' said Mum. 'That's why I don't want *anything* to go back to the way it was.'

My face fell. '... You don't?'

'No,' Mum smiled. 'I want it to be much better. I want to rebuild Middle Island. Not just our house – lots of houses. Maybe even a school, seeing as the Monster squashed your last one.'

I gasped. 'You mean we'll have *neighbours*?'

Mum nodded. 'Neighbours, pets ... we'll have them all!'

She held hands with me and Frank.

'*That's* why I wanted Frank here today – and every day after that. He's going to help us do it. Because sometimes family isn't enough. You need friends too. Good people. You need to have them around you all the time, even if you can't see them ...'

Suddenly the ceiling caved in and something landed in the middle of the table in a cloud of dust and foam insulation.

Fi apologised for sneaking into our air ducts at the station and for ruining our breakfast, but she explained that her cow-rustling had made her one of the most wanted criminals in the country and it was the only way she could get on board. She also said that a village on Middle Island sounded like a great idea, and that we could borrow her boat to transport stuff over from the mainland if we wanted, so long as we paid her an upfront deposit and a weekly rent thereafter, and so long as Mum adopted her.

Mum took a lot of convincing – partly because she didn't like the terms of the deal, but mainly because she had no idea who Fi was – but in the end, me and Frank talked her round.

'Fi's the smartest person I know!' I said. 'She can trick a whole roomful of people. Plus, she could tell that Mother actually wanted to sacrifice me.'

Mum frowned. 'Sacrifice? Caitlin, what on Earth are you . . .'

'And she's going to teach me to read, too!' I said. 'Please can you adopt her, Mum? Please please please?'

Mum didn't look too convinced. Frank put a hand on her shoulder.

'Emily – look, I know she seems like a sneaky little thief . . .'

'Oi,' said Fi.

'But she's a good person,' said Frank. 'She gave up everything she had to help Caitlin. She really does love her, you know.'

I beamed. 'That's right! We're friends.'

'*Best* friends,' said Fi.

We decided to celebrate our last night on the train before we got back to Middle Island. Frank bought a bottle of champagne and we all had some (even me!) and then I got dizzy and had to lie down. Mum did a dance and we managed to convince Frank to take his eye out. Fi showed us all how to pickpocket someone properly, but then Frank realised the wallet she was using was the one she'd stolen off him at the meeting, and Fi apologised and promised that from now on she was never going to steal anything ever again, but to be honest it was his own fault for keeping it in his back pocket anyway, and they were still arguing about it when I went to bed.

Actually, I didn't *really* go to bed. There was something that I wanted to do first. I made my way to the engineers' carriage, opened the hatch on the ceiling and climbed out onto the train roof.

Mum would have *killed* me if she knew – but then she doesn't need to know everything I do. I can do loads more than she thinks I can. That's what's different about me and Mum – she's amazing at the thinking side of things, which I'm not so great at. But I'm really good at *doing*.

I lay down on the carriage roof and looked up at the stars as the night slipped past. I love looking at them more than anything. I reckon it's where I do my best thinking – and I had lots to think about that night. I thought about how great it was that I suddenly had a whole family out of nowhere, and the best friends I could ever have asked for. I thought about how lucky I was.

And I thought about Perijee, of course. How could I not? I lay back and thought, *He's out there somewhere – under the ocean, where I can't see him.* Which sounds sad in some ways, but it's not really. Just because I can't see the bottom of the ocean, it doesn't mean it's not there. It's just hills and valleys covered in water.

I wondered where Perijee had ended up, and what was waiting for him back at his home. Maybe there were hundreds of other creatures like him down there – a family of his own, worried sick about him and wondering where he'd gone. Of course, I didn't know for sure – and I might never find out.

It's like the stars. You look up on any night and there's all of space, right ahead of you. Who *knows* what's out there that you can't see – there could be millions more Perijees, and billions of planets we've never seen, and trillions of people we haven't met, all dotted throughout the universe and looking back at the stars and wondering.

Which is a nice way to think about something that's normally a bit scary, isn't it? Space is the biggest thing you can imagine. It's so big and empty that it's easy to feel lonely when you look at it.

But I don't feel lonely when I look at it – not any more. Because no matter where I am, or where I go, or what I do, I know that there are people I love out there who are thinking of me.

And as for Perijee – well, I'm always thinking about him, too. There's not a single day that goes past where I don't miss him, and hope he's happy.

Otherwise, what's the point of being a friend?

ACKNOWLEDGEMENTS

The drawings at the beginning of each chapter were designed by children at the primary school where I teach. I asked them to imagine the numbers, letters and punctuation of an alien language, and then turn them into constellations. Some of the children were as young as five when they drew these; some were just leaving for secondary school.

Here are their names in the order their work appears in the book. I'm afraid I have no idea if their symbols are supposed to mean anything – you'll just have to ask them.

Ella Cawley, Jake Purton, Kira Westbrook, Yasmin Stopa, Poppy Williams, Evie Dooley, Nova-Leigh Canning, Charlotte Hamilton, Hanna Brighi, Sari Robinson, Ella Munro-Peebles, Zara Sprange, Eabha Brady, Martha Beavan, Enid O'Rourke, James Crowther, Tilley Du Preez, Oluwaleke Ayoade, Chloe Phillips, Toby Hamilton, Jemimah Alloo, Lukas Persson, Eva Elias, Sunday Wood, Miran Allak, Emily Coles, Joseph Harvey, Iris Pendlebury.

Sorry it took so long, guys – I'm a really slow writer.